W9-BOE-661

FARRAR
STRAUS
GIROUX

THE
CHRISTMAS
MYSTERY

ALSO BY JOSTEIN GAARDER

Sophie's World

The Solitaire Mystery

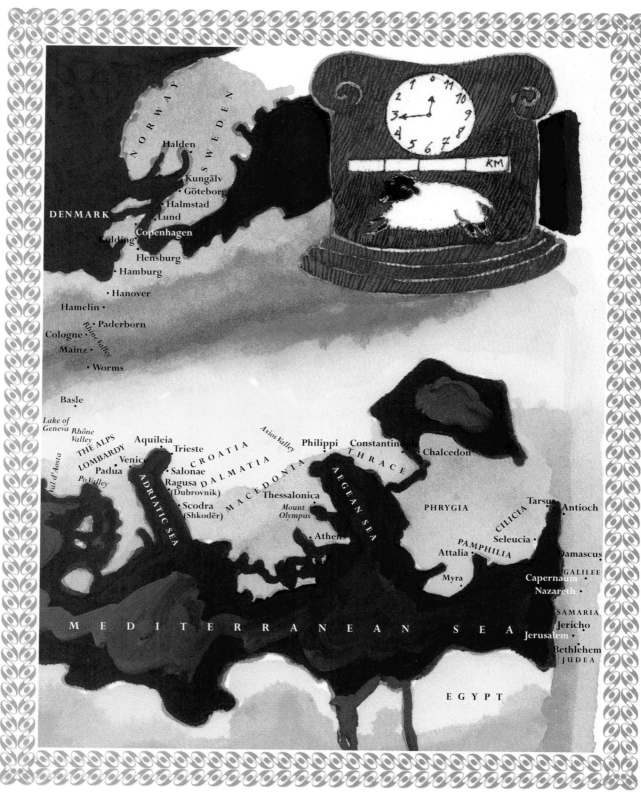

THE

CHRISTMAS

MYSTERY

JOSTEIN GAARDER

Decorations by

ROSEMARY WELLS

Translated by Elizabeth Rokkan

FARRAR STRAUS GIROUX

NEW YORK

Translation copyright © 1996 by Elizabeth Rokkan
Illustrations © 1996 by Rosemary Wells
All rights reserved
Originally published in Norwegian under the title *Julemysteriet*,
copyright © 1992 by H. Aschehoug & Co. (W. Nygaard), Oslo
Printed in the United States of America
Published simultaneously in Canada by HarperCollins*CanadaLtd*
Design by Fritz Metsch
First printing, 1996

LIBRARY OF CONGRESS CATALOGING-IN-PUBLICATION DATA
Gaarder, Jostein.
[Julemysteriet. English]
The Christmas mystery / Jostein Gaarder ; decorations by Rosemary
Wells ; translated by Elizabeth Rokkan.
p.   cm.
[1. Christmas—Fiction.   2. Advent—Fiction.   3. Time travel—
Fiction.   4. Jesus Christ—Nativity—Fiction.]   I. Wells,
Rosemary, ill.   II. Rokkan, Elizabeth.   III. Title.
PZ7.G1114Ch   1996   [Fic]—dc20   96-27916   CIP   AC

❧ CONTENTS ❧

THE CHRISTMAS MYSTERY

❈ DECEMBER 1 ❈

. . . perhaps the clock hands had become
so tired of going in the same direction year after
year that they had suddenly begun to
go the opposite way instead . . .

DUSK was falling. The lights were on in the Christmas streets, and thick snowflakes danced between the lamps. The streets were crowded with people.

Among all these busy people were Papa and Joachim. They had gone into town to buy an Advent calendar, and it was their last chance, because tomorrow would be December 1. They were sold out at the newsstand and in the big bookstore in the market square.

Joachim tugged Papa's hand hard and pointed to a tiny shop window. An Advent calendar in bright colors was leaning against a pile of books. "There!" he said.

Papa turned back. "Saved!"

They went into the tiny bookshop. Joachim thought it looked a little old and worn out. There were shelves from floor to ceiling along all the walls, and on all the shelves the books were tightly packed. Almost no two were alike.

A large pile of Advent calendars lay on the counter. There were two kinds. One had a picture of Santa Claus with a sled and reindeer; the other had a picture of a barn with a tiny Christmas elf, a *nisse*, eating porridge out of a big bowl.

Papa held up the two calendars. "There are chocolates behind the doors in this one," he said, "but, of course, your dentist wouldn't like that very much. The other has small plastic figures."

Joachim examined the two calendars. He didn't know which one he wanted.

"It was different when I was a boy," said Papa.

"What do you mean?"

"Then there was only a tiny picture behind each door, one for each day. We were so excited every morning! We used to try to guess what the picture would be. Then we opened the door . . . well, we *opened* it, you see. It was like opening the door to a different world."

Joachim had noticed something. He pointed to a wall of books. "There's an Advent calendar over there, too."

He ran over to get it and held it up to show Papa. It had a picture of Joseph and Mary bending over the Baby Jesus in the manger. The Three Wise Men from the East were kneeling in the background. Outside the stable were the shepherds with their sheep, and angels floated down from the sky. One of them was blowing a trumpet.

The calendar's colors were faded, as if it had been lying in the sun all summer. But the picture was so beautiful that Joachim almost felt a little sorry for it.

"I want this one," he said.

Papa smiled. "You know, I don't think this one's for sale. I think it must be very old. Maybe as old as I am."

Joachim wouldn't give up. "None of the doors are open."

"But it's only here for decoration."

Joachim hadn't taken his eyes off the calendar. "I want it," he repeated. "I want the one that's like none of the others."

The bookseller, an older man with white hair, came over. He looked surprised when he saw the Advent calendar.

"Beautiful!" he exclaimed. "And genuine—yes, original. It almost looks homemade."

"He wants to buy it," said Papa, gesturing toward Joachim. "I'm trying to explain that it's not for sale."

The white-haired man raised his eyebrows. "Did you find it here? I haven't seen one like that for many, many years."

"It was in front of all the books," said Joachim, pointing.

The bookseller nodded. "Oh, old John must be up to his tricks again."

Papa stared. "John?"

"Yes, he's a strange character. He sells roses in the market. Sometimes he comes in and asks for a glass of water. In summer when it's hot he'll pour the last drops over his head before he goes out again. He's poured a few drops over me a couple of times, too. To thank me for the water, he sometimes leaves one or two roses on the counter; or he'll put an old book on the bookshelf. Once he put a photograph of a young woman in the window. It was from a country far away. Maybe that's where he comes from himself. 'Elisabet,' it said on the photo."

"And now he's left an Advent calendar?" Papa asked.

"Yes, apparently."

"There's something written on it," said Joachim. He read aloud: "MAGIC ADVENT CALENDAR. Price: 75 øre."

The bookseller nodded. "In that case, it must be very old."

"May I buy it for 75 øre?" asked Joachim.

The man laughed. "I think you should have it for nothing. You'll see, old John had you in mind."

"Thank you, thank you, thank you," said Joachim. He was already on his way out of the bookshop.

Papa shook the bookseller's hand and followed Joachim out to the side-walk.

Joachim hugged the calendar tight. "I'll open the first door tomorrow," he said.

JOACHIM woke up many times that night. He thought about the white-haired bookseller and about John with his roses at the market. He went to the bathroom and drank water from the tap. He remembered that John had poured water over his head.

Most of all, he thought about the magic Advent calendar which was as old as Papa. And yet nobody had opened any of the doors. Before he went to bed, he found all the doors, from 1 to 24. The twenty-fourth was, of course, Christmas Eve, and that door was four times bigger than the others. It covered almost the entire manger in the stable.

Where had the Advent calendar been for over forty years? And what would happen when he opened the first door, in a little while? He and Papa had hung the calendar on a hook above his bed.

When he woke up again, it was seven o'clock. He reached up and tried to open the first door, but his fingers were so impatient that it was difficult to hold it properly. At last he managed to loosen a tiny corner, and the door opened slowly.

Joachim gazed at a picture of a toy store. Among all the toys and the people were a little lamb and a small girl, but he couldn't look more closely at the picture because, just as he opened the door, something fell out on his bed. He picked it up.

It was a thin sheet of paper, folded over and over. He smoothed it out and saw that there was writing on both sides. He began to read.

THE LITTLE LAMB

"Elisabet!" her mother called after her. "Come back, Elisabet!"

Elisabet Hansen had been standing staring at the big pile of teddy bears and stuffed animals while her mother was buying Christmas presents for the cousins who lived in Toten. All of a sudden, a little lamb popped out of the pile, jumped to the floor, and looked around. It had a bell around its neck, and the bell started to jingle in competition with all the cash registers.

How could a toy suddenly come to life? Elisabet was so surprised that she started to chase the lamb. It was running across the floor of the department store in the direction of the escalator.

"Little lamb, little lamb!" she called after it.

The lamb was now on the escalator, which led to the floor below. The escalator moved quickly, and the lamb leaped even faster, so that Elisabet had to run faster than the escalator and the lamb together to catch up with it.

"Come back, Elisabet!" repeated her mother, severely.

But Elisabet had already jumped on the escalator. She could see the lamb running across the ground floor, where they sold underwear and ties.

As soon as she had solid ground beneath her feet again, she went the same way as the lamb. It had bounded out to the street, where the snowflakes were dancing amid all the strings of Christmas lights hanging from the streetlights. Elisabet knocked over a display of winter gloves and followed it.

The street was so noisy that she could only just hear the bell jingling over on Church Road. But Elisabet did not give up. She was determined to pat the lamb's soft fleece.

"Little lamb, little lamb!"

The lamb dashed across the road against the light. Perhaps it thought a red man on the traffic light meant "Go!" and a green man meant "Stop!" Elisabet thought she had heard that sheep were color-blind. At any rate, the lamb didn't stop at the red man on the light, so Elisabet couldn't stop either. She was going to catch up with the lamb even if she had to follow it to the ends of the earth.

The cars honked their horns, and a motorcycle had to swerve onto the sidewalk to avoid colliding with Elisabet or with the little lamb. The people doing their Christmas shopping stared. They didn't often see a little girl running across Church Road against the light to catch a lamb. In any case, it was unusual to be running after a lamb in the middle of winter.

As they ran, Elisabet heard the church clock strike three. She noticed it especially, because she knew she had come to town on the five o'clock bus. Perhaps the clock hands had become so tired of going in the same direction year after year that they had suddenly begun to go the opposite way instead. Elisabet thought that clocks, too, might get bored with doing the same thing all the time.

But there was something else. When Elisabet had gone into the department store, it had been almost completely dark outside. Now it was light again, and that was odd, because there had been no night in between.

As soon as the lamb had the chance, it turned onto a road leading out of town and trotted on toward some woods. It leaped onto a path between tall pine trees. Now it had to slow down a little, because the path was covered with the snow that had been falling during the past few days.

Elisabet went after it. It was difficult for her to run, too. But the lamb had four legs that were dragging in the snow, while she had only two. Perhaps that would help her to catch up.

Her mother's cries had been drowned long ago by the noise in the street. Soon she couldn't even hear street sounds. But something was still singing in her ears: "Should we buy this one or that one? What do you think, Elisabet?"

Perhaps the lamb had come to life and run away from the big store because it could not bear to listen to all the cash registers and all the talk about buying and selling. And perhaps that was why Elisabet was following it. She had never been very fond of shopping.

☽ ☆

JOACHIM looked up from the thin sheet of paper that had fallen out of the magic Advent calendar. He was amazed by what he had read.

He had always liked secrets. Now he remembered the little box with the key in it, the one Grandma had bought him in Poland. Mama and Papa had made him a solemn promise that they would never look for the key and open the box when Joachim was asleep or at school. It would be as bad as opening someone else's letters, they had said.

Until today, Joachim hadn't had any real secrets to hide in the box. But now he put the paper from the Advent calendar there, locked it up, and hid the key under his pillow. When Mama and Papa woke up and came to look at the Advent calendar, too, they would see only the picture of the lamb in the department store.

"Do you remember?" asked Mama, looking up at Papa. "It was just like that when we were small."

Papa nodded. "Then we used our imagination and made up a story about each little picture. It was much better than plastic figures that end up being swallowed by an angry vaccuum cleaner."

Joachim was laughing inside. Only he knew that there had been a mysterious piece of paper inside the calendar.

He pointed to the picture of the lamb. "The lamb has decided to run away from the shop," he said, "because it can't bear listening to all the cash registers and all the talk of buying and selling. But there's a little girl called Elisabet in the shop, and she runs after the lamb because she wants to pat its soft fleece."

"See what I mean?" Papa said. "What does the boy want with plastic figures?"

For the rest of the day, Joachim wondered whether Elisabet would catch up with the lamb so that she could pat its fleece. Would he find out tomorrow?

For then surely there would be another thin piece of paper.

2

*. . . I know a short cut, and that's the path
we're taking now . . .*

JOACHIM woke up before Mama and Papa the next morning, too, but he nearly always did. He sat up and looked at the big Advent calendar.

Only now did he notice a little lamb lying at the feet of one of the shepherds. Wasn't that strange? He had looked at the large picture with all the angels and the Wise Men, the shepherds and the sheep, many, many times. But he hadn't seen the little lamb until now.

Perhaps it was because he had read about the lamb on the piece of paper that had fallen out of the calendar.

But that lamb had jumped out of a modern store—and the lamb on the Advent calendar had lived in Bethlehem long, long ago. There were no cars and no traffic lights then and no big stores with escalators and cash registers. Besides, Elisabet had heard the church clock striking three, and surely there were no church clocks two thousand years ago? Joachim knew that it was as long ago as that since the Baby Jesus was born.

Now he found the door with the number 2 on it, and opened it carefully. A folded piece of paper fell out of the calendar as the door opened. He peeped in at a picture of some woods. Among the trees was an angel with his arm around a little girl.

Joachim unfolded the paper and saw that there was writing on it in tiny letters on both sides. He began to read.

EPHIRIEL

Elisabet Hansen didn't know how far or how long she had been running after the little lamb. But when she set off through the town it had been snowing heavily. Now it had not only stopped snowing; there was no snow on the path at all. Among the trees she could see blue anemones, coltsfoot, and windflowers, and that was unusual, since it was right before Christmas.

She picked an anemone and looked at the blue petals carefully. Picking flowers at this time of year was every bit as mysterious as it would have been to throw snowballs in midsummer.

It occurred to Elisabet that perhaps she had run so far that she had reached a country where it was summer all year round. If not, she must have run so long that spring and the warm weather had already arrived. In that case, she might still be in Norway, but then, what would have happened to Christmas?

While she stood wondering, she heard the tinkle of a bell far away. Elisabet started running again and soon saw the lamb. It had found a small grassy hillside and was grazing greedily.

That was not particularly surprising, for the little creature had probably been very hungry. It had not had any grass to eat as long as it was winter. It had certainly not had so much as a morsel of food as long as it had been a toy either, and that may have been for a very long time.

Elisabet crept toward the lamb, but just as she was about to pounce on it in order to pat its fleece, it leaped away again.

"Little lamb, little lamb!"

Elisabet tried to keep up with it, but she tripped over a pine-tree root and fell flat on the ground.

The worst thing wasn't that she had hurt herself, but that she realized she probably wouldn't ever catch up with the lamb. She had decided to follow it to the ends of the earth, but the earth was round, after all, so they might go on running around the world forever, or at least until she grew up, and by then she might have lost interest in lambs and the like.

When she looked up, she saw a shining figure between the trees. Elisabet stared, wide-eyed, because it was neither an animal nor a human being. A pair of wings were sticking out of a robe as white as the lamb.

Elisabet was only just getting to know the world. She knew what the most common animals were called, but she hadn't learned the difference between a tomtit and a yellowhammer, for example. Or between a camel and a dromedary, come to think of it. Still, there was no mistaking what she was looking at now. Elisabet understood at once that the shining figure must be an angel. She had seen angels in books, but it was the first time she had seen such a creature in real life.

"Fear not!" said the angel in a gentle voice.

Elisabet raised herself halfway up. "Don't think I'm afraid of you," she said, sulking a little because she had fallen and hurt herself.

The angel came closer. It looked as if he was hovering just above the ground. He reminded Elisabet of her Cousin Anna, who could dance on the tips of her toes. The angel knelt down and stroked Elisabet gently on the nape of her neck with the tip of one of his wings.

"I said, 'Fear not,' to be on the safe side," he said. "We don't appear to humans very often, so it's best to be careful when we do. Usually people are very frightened when they're visited by an angel."

Suddenly Elisabet began to cry, not because she was afraid of angels, and not because she had hurt herself, either. She didn't understand why she was crying until she heard herself sob, "I wanted . . . to pet the lamb."

The angel nodded gracefully. "I'm sure God wouldn't have created lambs with such soft fleece unless He hoped someone would want to pet them."

"The lamb runs much faster than I do," said Elisabet, sobbing, "and it has twice as many legs . . . Isn't that unfair? I can't see why a little lamb should be in such a hurry."

The angel helped her to her feet and said confidentially, "It's going to Bethlehem."

Elisabet had stopped crying. "To Bethlehem?"

"Yes. To Bethlehem, to Bethlehem! That's where Jesus was born."

Elisabet was very surprised at what the angel said. In an attempt to hide her astonishment, she began to brush dirt and grass off her pants. There were some nasty stains on her red jacket, too.

"Then I want to go to Bethlehem," she said.

The angel had begun dancing on the tips of his toes again on the path. "That suits me," he said, hovering just above the ground, "because I'm going there, too. So we might just as well keep each other company, all three of us."

Elisabet had been taught that she should never go anywhere with people she didn't know. That certainly applied to angels and trolls as well. She looked up at the angel and asked, "What's your name?"

She had thought that the angel was a man, but she wasn't quite sure. Now he curtsied like a ballet dancer and said, "My name is Ephiriel."

"That sounds like a butterfly. Did you really say Ephiriel?"

The angel nodded. "Just Ephiriel, yes. Angels have no mother or father, so we have no family name."

Elisabet sniffed for the last time. Then she said, "I don't think we have time to talk anymore if we're going all the way to Bethlehem. Isn't it far away?"

"Yes indeed, it's very far—and a very long time ago. But I know a short cut, and that's the path we're taking now."

And, with that, they began to run. First the lamb, then Elisabet. The angel Ephiriel danced behind them.

As they ran, Elisabet wished she had asked the angel why it had suddenly become summer. But when she caught a glimpse of the lamb on the path in front of her, she didn't dare stop.

"Little lamb, little lamb!"

☽ ☆

JOACHIM quickly hid the piece of paper in the secret box.

It was John the flower seller who had left the old calendar with the bookseller. Did he know about the scraps of paper, too? Or was Joachim the only person in the world who knew the secret? After all, he was the only person who had opened the calendar.

Another thought struck him. Elisabet! Wasn't Elisabet the name of the woman whose picture John had put in the shop window?

Yes, it was, he was certain. Could it be the same Elisabet he was reading about in the magic Advent calendar? She was only a child, it's true, but the calendar was so old that she must have had plenty of time to grow up during all the years that had passed since then.

Mama and Papa came in that day, too, to see the picture in the calendar.

"An angel," whispered Mama solemnly.

"He's comforting Elisabet," explained Joachim. "She was running so fast after the lamb that she fell and hurt herself."

Mama winked at Papa, and Papa smiled shyly. It was probably because they thought Joachim was good at inventing stories. They didn't know that he wasn't inventing anything at all.

That day he had to get to school early, so there was no more time to talk about the Advent calendar. But Joachim thought about nothing else on his way there.

When he came home from school, he had to let himself in. He got home a little earlier than Mama nearly every day.

Joachim rushed to his room and looked up at the magic Advent calendar. It was still there. He had had to ask himself a couple of times during the day whether it had been only a dream, because Joachim was always dreaming about the strangest things.

He longed to know what the picture behind door number 3 was. Should he open the third door? All he had to do was push it back again afterwards and pretend he hadn't done it.

But that would be cheating. You weren't allowed to cheat at cards either, but it would be even worse to cheat about Christmas. It was like peeping into presents that were not to be opened until Christmas Eve. It was almost like stealing from yourself.

Mama soon came home from work and started to peel potatoes and carrots.

Then Papa arrived. He was complaining that he had lost his driver's license.

"I can't understand it," he said. "Not in the car, not at the office, and not in my coat pocket, either."

"What a muddlehead you are!" said Joachim. Because Papa always said that to him when he couldn't find his pencil case or he hadn't put his toys away.

That evening must have been the first time in Joachim's whole life that he asked to go to bed early.

"You don't feel ill, do you, darling?" asked Mama.

"No, of course not. But the sooner I go to sleep, the sooner I will wake up to open the magic Advent calendar."

❧ DECEMBER 3 ❧

*. . . like running before
the wind—or like rushing down
an escalator . . .*

JOACHIM woke up early on December 3. The Donald Duck clock hanging above his desk said a quarter to seven. Mama and Papa would not be up for another half hour.

He remembered that he'd dreamed about something strange, but he was not quite sure what. It had had something to do with the angel Ephiriel and the lamb.

He sat up in bed and looked closely at the magic Advent calendar. At the top of the picture, several angels were floating down through the clouds in the sky. One of them was blowing a trumpet. That was to wake up all the sheep and the shepherds, of course.

Joachim imagined that the angel on the right of the picture must be the angel Ephiriel. He looked just like Joachim thought Ephiriel might look.

Suddenly he noticed that that angel was smiling at him, lifting an arm as if trying to wave at Joachim. The angel in the picture looked clearer than yesterday.

Joachim got up on the bed and opened the door with the number 3 on it. He saw a tiny picture of a vintage car. He had seen that kind of old car at the Technical Museum with Grandpa.

Joachim didn't understand what a vintage car could have to do with Christmas, but he picked up the thin sheet of paper that had fallen out of the calendar. He snuggled down under the covers and began to read.

THE SECOND SHEEP

Elisabet and the angel Ephiriel went on running after the little lamb. Soon they left the woods behind and were going down a narrow country lane. In the distance, thick smoke rose from some tall factory chimneys.

"There's a town," said Elisabet.

"That's Halden," explained the angel. "We're fairly close to Sweden."

Suddenly they heard a clatter right behind them. Elisabet turned and saw an old car heading toward them. In the car sat a man wearing a hat and a coat. He had a black beard and looked a little like the picture of her great-grandfather on the mantelpiece at home. As the car passed them, the man honked the horn and saluted with his hat.

"Look at that car!" exclaimed Elisabet. "It must be really old."

"On the contrary, I think it was probably brand-new," said Ephiriel.

Elisabet sighed. "I've always thought angels were much cleverer than humans. But you don't seem to know much about cars."

Still, she didn't want to quarrel with the angel, so she went on, "But

I suppose you don't drive cars in heaven. I imagine God has forbidden any kind of pollution."

Ephiriel pointed to a large pile of logs. "Sit down here," he said. "You deserve a short rest, and there's something important I have to tell you about our journey to Bethlehem."

Elisabet sat down and looked up at the angel. "Don't you get tired, too?" she asked.

The angel shook his head. "No, angels don't get tired, because we're not made of flesh and blood. When you get tired, it's your flesh and blood that feel it most."

Elisabet felt a little embarrassed that she had thought angels could get tired. If they had been able to, they surely wouldn't have the strength to fly up and down between heaven and earth. That must be very far, maybe even farther than Bethlehem.

"Exactly where are we going, my dear?" asked the angel.

"To Bethlehem," replied Elisabet.

"Very well, and what are we going to do there?"

"We're going to pet the lamb."

The angel nodded. "And we'll welcome the Baby Jesus into the world. He was called God's lamb. That was because He was just as kind and as innocent as a little lamb's fleece is soft."

Elisabet shrugged. This was something she'd never thought about.

"But it's not enough just to travel to Bethlehem," the angel continued. "We have to travel two thousand years back in time, too. That's because when you started to run after the lamb, just about that length of time had passed since Jesus was born. We'll try to get there at the moment when the great wonder happens."

"Isn't it absolutely impossible to travel back in time?" Elisabet asked.

Ephiriel shook his head. "Not absolutely, no. Nothing is impossible for God, and I'm here as God's messenger, so practically nothing is impossible for me, either. We have a small part of the long way behind us already. Down there you see Halden, and we're at the beginning of the twentieth century after Jesus' birth. Can you understand that?"

Elisabet's eyes widened, and she nodded. "I think so—and that means the vintage car wasn't so old, after all."

"No. It may have been brand-new. I'm sure you noticed how proud the driver was when he honked his horn. Not very many people own cars at this time."

Elisabet simply sat and stared, and the angel Ephiriel continued. "It would have taken a very long time to run to Bethlehem in a straight line. But we're also running diagonally down through history, so in a way we're going downhill all the time. It's like running before the wind—or like rushing down an escalator."

Elisabet nodded. She was not at all sure she understood everything the angel said, but she understood enough to realize how clever it all was.

"How do you know we're at the beginning of the twentieth century?"

The angel raised his arm and pointed at a gold watch on his wrist. It was decorated with a row of shining pearls. On its face it said 1916.

"It's an angel watch," he explained. "It isn't quite as accurate as other watches, but in heaven we're not too particular about all those hours and minutes."

"Why not?"

"We have the whole of eternity to see to," replied the angel. "Besides, we never have to catch a bus to get to work on time."

Now Elisabet understood why the church clock had only struck three even though it had been six or seven o'clock when she ran from the shop and why the snow had disappeared and it had suddenly become summer. She had run backward in time.

"You began running along the diagonal path as soon as you started chasing the lamb," continued the angel Ephiriel. "That's when the long journey through time and space began."

Another car approached them from the opposite direction. It left such a cloud of dust and sand behind it that it made Elisabet cough.

When the dust cloud had settled, she pointed up at the road. "There's our lamb again. But now there's a grown sheep as well."

The angel nodded. "Verily I say unto you, that sheep is going to Bethlehem, too."

With that, they began to run. When Elisabet and Ephiriel had caught up with the lamb and the sheep, both of them bounded on as well.

"Little lamb, little lamb!" coaxed Elisabet.

But the lamb and the sheep would not be coaxed into standing still. They were going to Bethlehem! To Bethlehem!

They passed the outskirts of Halden. They paused for a moment and looked down at all the people walking in the streets and the market. The ladies were wearing long, colorful cotton dresses and large hats. Several vintage cars were sputtering along the streets, but there were horses and carriages as well.

They left it behind them and soon came to a border station. A large sign announced: "Border. SWEDEN."

Elisabet stopped abruptly. "Do you think we'll be allowed to go into Sweden?"

The angel fluttered around her like an overgrown butterfly. "They won't dare stop a pilgrimage," he replied. "Besides, it's only a few weeks since Norway had the same king as Sweden."

"May I look at your angel watch again?"

Ephiriel stretched out his arm. The watch said 1905.

Then they sped past two border guards, the lamb and the sheep first, and Elisabet Hansen and the angel Ephiriel just behind them.

"Halt!" shouted the border guards. "In the name of the law."

But they were already far into Sweden. And they had come a few years closer to the birth of Jesus.

☽ ☆

JOACHIM sat up in bed. So that was why there was a picture of a vintage car in the Advent calendar! That was why it had suddenly become summer.

Joachim quickly locked the piece of paper with the story of Elisabet and the angel Ephiriel in the secret box. Afterwards, he sat for a long time, thinking over what he had read.

Elisabet hadn't just set off after the lamb and followed it into the woods. She had begun to run back in time as well. She had already come to the year 1905, but she was going all the way to Bethlehem when Jesus was born. Joachim knew that it happened almost two thousand years ago.

He was old enough to know that you can't really run back in time. But it was possible to do it in your thoughts.

At school he had heard that a thousand years to mankind can be as one single day to God. And the angel Ephiriel had told Elisabet that nothing is impossible for God. Could Elisabet and the angel really have run back in time?

He heard Mama on the landing. She came into his room and asked, "Have you opened the Advent calendar?"

He nodded, and Mama looked at the picture in the calendar. "A vintage car!" she exclaimed.

She sounded surprised, almost disappointed. Perhaps she thought there should be pictures of angels and Christmasy things every day.

"It's because Elisabet and the angel Ephiriel have run to Sweden at the time when vintage cars like that were brand-new," said Joachim. "They're going to run all the way to Bethlehem."

"You're a real little storyteller," said Mama, patting him on the head. Then she went into the bathroom.

Joachim felt a tickle in his stomach when he thought about all the clever things he knew about which Mama and Papa believed he was just making up. He decided something even cleverer. On Christmas Eve he'd put together all the pieces of paper that had come from the magic calendar and place the package under the Christmas tree. Then he would write: "To the best Mama and Papa in the world" on the outside.

This idea made him look forward to Christmas even more. But it wasn't always good to look forward to something. It could be boring, too, if it took a long time to come. When he looked forward to something terribly exciting, it could almost give him a headache.

That afternoon, Papa complained that he still hadn't found his driver's license. In that case, he wasn't really supposed to drive, said Mama. But when Papa heard that, he snorted like a steam engine.

❧ DECEMBER 4 ❧

. . . he barely had time to look astonished . . .

WHEN Joachim woke up on Friday, he made sure it was completely quiet in the house. Then he opened the fourth door.

It was a picture of a man in a light blue robe which looked a little like a nightgown. In his hand he held a tall staff. But Joachim had no time to look at the picture carefully, because a scrap of paper fell on his bed today, too.

JOSHUA

Elisabet Hansen and the angel Ephiriel hurried after the sheep and the lamb. They passed a red log cabin in a small clearing in the woods.

From a hilltop, Ephiriel pointed down at a large lake. "That's Vänern, the biggest lake in Scandinavia," he said. "The watch shows that 1891 years have passed since Jesus was born, but we've only just arrived in Sweden."

A rapidly moving river flowed out of the lake. A bridge arched over the river, and they walked across it to the other side.

"This is the Göta River," said Ephiriel. "We'll follow an old cart track along the riverbank."

"Little lamb, little lamb!" coaxed Elisabet, but the sheep and the lamb were already running again.

They passed a village. On the outskirts was a church that was painted red, and the people from the village were heading along the road toward it. Most of them were on foot, but some of them sat in big, horse-drawn carts. The men were dressed in black suits and black hats, and many of the women were in black as well. Some of them carried hymn books.

"It must be Sunday," said Elisabet.

They paused for a moment or two and looked down at all the people. Suddenly a little boy noticed them, but he barely had time to look astonished, because at that same moment the angel Ephiriel began running again. Elisabet had to hurry to keep up. Once she turned and looked back, but all the people in front of the church had vanished. The horses and carts had vanished, too.

When they left the village behind, Elisabet turned to the angel and said, "The only one who saw us was a little boy."

"Excellent. We try not to attract too much attention. Sometimes we can't help it if someone catches sight of us, but a glimpse is quite enough."

They ran on through woods and fields. Now and again, they saw people making hay or reaping wheat with scythes. Sometimes they had to take a roundabout way so as not to scare anyone.

Before long, the sheep and the lamb found a field that was so green and tempting that it dazzled the eyes.

"Now's our chance," whispered Elisabet, "if we go up to them carefully."

But just then a man came walking toward them. He was wearing a blue tunic, and holding a tall staff that was curved at the top. He greeted them. "Peace be with you who walk on the narrow way along the Göta River. My name is Joshua the shepherd."

"Then you are one of us," said Ephiriel.

Elisabet didn't understand what the angel meant by that. But then the shepherd said, "I am coming with you to the Holy Land, for I must be in the fields when the angels announce the glad tidings of the birth of Jesus."

A clever idea occurred to Elisabet. "If you are a proper shepherd, perhaps you can bring the lamb to me?"

The shepherd bowed low. "That's not difficult for a good shepherd."

He took a few steps firmly toward the sheep and the lamb. The next moment, the lamb was lying at Elisabet's feet. She knelt and petted its soft fleece. "I think you are the fastest stuffed animal in the world," she said, "but I caught you at last!"

The shepherd thumped his crook on the ground and said, "To Bethlehem! To Bethlehem!"

The lamb and the sheep bounded away, the shepherd, the angel, and Elisabet after them.

They came to another small town. From a hill outside the town, they looked down on a cluster of red timber houses. Ephiriel explained that the town was called Kungälv.

"That means Kings' Rock. The town was given that name because the Scandinavian kings used to meet here to take counsel together. One of them was Sigurd Jorsalfar. Jorsalfar means the pilgrimage to Jerusalem. Sigurd was given that name because he had gone on a pilgrimage to the Holy Land where Jesus was born."

Soon they passed above a city at the mouth of the Göta River. Women in long dresses and men wearing hats and carrying walking sticks were parading up and down the streets. Others rode in fine coaches drawn by two horses.

"That's Göteborg," said Ephiriel. "The time is 1814, and Denmark has had to hand Norway over to Sweden. Now Norway will get her own Constitution."

Joshua the shepherd turned and waved to them. "To Bethlehem!" he called. "To Bethlehem!"

They sped on through Sweden.

☽ ☆

JOACHIM had just hidden the paper from the Advent calendar in his secret box when Mama came into his room.

"And what was the picture today?" she asked.

Joachim knew he did not need to answer. Mama always wanted to look for herself.

She clasped her hands. "It must be one of the shepherds in the fields."

"Why do you say 'in the fields'?" asked Joachim.

Mama told him that there were pictures of shepherds in nice old Advent calendars because an angel had come to the shepherds in the fields to tell them that the Baby Jesus was born.

"They've come as far as Göteborg," explained Joachim.

"Göteborg?" Mama looked at him oddly. "Who are 'they'?"

"Elisabet Hansen, the angel Ephiriel, and Joshua the shepherd. They're going to Bethlehem! To Bethlehem!"

Mama looked at him in astonishment. "Don't let this old calendar get to you. They're only pictures."

Joachim realized that he couldn't keep telling Mama and Papa all he knew about Elisabet. If he did, he wouldn't be able to keep the secret of the scraps of paper in the calendar either.

He realized something else, too. He would have to try to talk to John. John was the only person who knew where the magic Advent calendar had come from. Perhaps he also knew more about Elisabet Hansen. But how could Joachim find John? He wasn't allowed to go to town and to the market square by himself.

He had just come home from school that afternoon when someone rang the doorbell. It couldn't be Mama, because she knew Joachim never locked the door from the inside. So who could it be?

He went out into the hall and opened the door. On the steps stood the bookseller who had given him the Advent calendar!

"Ah, there you are," he said. "Just as I thought."

"Why?" asked Joachim, suddenly a little scared that the bookseller might have come to ask for the magic Advent calendar back.

Besides, how did he know where they lived?

The man put his hand into his coat pocket and took out a driver's license.

"Your father left this on the counter," he explained. "I thought it must be yours, but since you didn't come back to the store I decided to drop it off myself. I live close by, you see, at 12 Clover Road."

That wasn't far. One of Joachim's classmates lived at number 7.

"And how's it going with the magic Advent calendar?" asked the bookseller.

"Super," said Joachim. "There are some mysterious pieces of paper in it, too."

"Are there?"

The bookseller gave him a big smile. He handed Joachim Papa's driver's license. "Well, I must be going on," he said. "It's a busy time for us booksellers."

It wasn't long before Mama and Papa came home from work. Shortly afterwards, they had dinner.

Joachim had decided not to say anything about the driver's license until Papa mentioned it himself.

Instead, he started to talk about something completely different. "What's a pilgrimage?"

His parents must have thought it strange that Joachim asked about that, because "pilgrimage" was a difficult word. Papa helped himself to more fish pie and said, "A pilgrim is someone who travels to a holy place."

"Like Sigurd Jorsalfar?" asked Joachim. "He traveled all the way to Jerusalem, didn't he? That's why he was called the Traveler to Jerusalem."

Mama and Papa looked at each other. "Have you been learning about Sigurd Jorsalfar at school?" asked Mama.

Joachim shook his head. He realized it was time to talk about the driver's license. He looked up at Papa. "Have you found your driver's license yet?"

"Not a trace," said Papa.

"I have," said Joachim.

He got up from his chair and went into his room to get the driver's license. He handed it to Papa, smiling mischievously.

Papa nearly choked on his dinner. "Where did you find it, Joachim? Surely *you* didn't——"

Joachim had to interrupt Papa before he said something he would come to regret. "You left it in the bookshop when we bought the Advent calendar."

Papa looked as if he had had a visitation from an angel in broad daylight. He had in a way, too, except that the angel had sent a white-haired bookseller instead of coming himself.

"He came this afternoon," explained Joachim. "He said he lives nearby."

Then Mama and Papa understood.

"Well, he's quite a bookseller," said Papa. He turned to Mama. "That is quite unusual."

"And you're quite an unusual muddlehead," said Joachim.

5

❧ DECEMBER 5 ❧

. . ."a thousand ages
in thy sight are like an evening gone" . . .

JOACHIM was glad there were no chocolates or plastic figures in the old Advent calendar. But Papa had not been right when he said there were only pictures behind the doors.

A strange story was hidden inside the magic Advent calendar. It took 24 days to read the whole of the tale, since the story was divided into 24 small chapters, one for each day. Each day, another pilgrim joined the pilgrimage.

December 5 was a Saturday. Mama and Papa usually slept late on the weekends. Joachim woke up at seven, as he always did. He sat up in bed and examined the big picture on the calendar.

Only now did he see that one of the shepherds was holding a crook in his hand—just like Joshua.

Why hadn't he noticed that before?

Every time he looked at the magic calendar, he discovered something new. But surely there couldn't be anything more to see than what had been there all the time? Wouldn't that be like a magic trick?

Amazed, Joachim took a deep breath.

Perhaps that was what made the old Advent calendar magical? The picture outside had never been completely finished, and gradually what was missing was painted in as the doors were opened and the pieces of paper were read.

Was it really possible to make a picture like that?

Joachim knew that bread was not quite ready until it had risen all by itself—first in the baking pan and then in the oven. He knew that it had something to do with yeast, because Joachim had often helped Mama or Papa bake bread. When he was smaller, he used to think that babies inside their mothers' stomachs must be like yeast.

Wasn't the whole world a magic picture which added to itself? For the world changed all the time. It was never completely finished.

If God had made a whole world that could create itself in every tiny nook and cranny, then He could probably manage to make a picture that developed itself in front of the eyes of those looking at it.

Joachim opened the door with the number 5 on it. Today's picture was of a rowboat. In it sat a shepherd, an angel, a little girl, and three sheep. Joachim knew who they were, but what interested him most was the thin sheet of paper.

THE THIRD SHEEP

Elisabet, the lamb, the angel, the sheep, and the shepherd sped through Sweden along dirt roads and grassy cart tracks, between yellow fields and through dense forests, until they looked out over a little town down by the sea. The wind blew so strongly that the waves were breaking over the line of the pier. Far out to sea, there was a sailing ship with three tall masts. At the edge of the town was a large castle.

"We are in Halland," said the angel Ephiriel. "The town is called

Halmstad, and the waves are rolling in from Kattegat. The watch says that 1789 years have passed since Jesus was born."

"Are we still in Sweden?" asked Elisabet.

Ephiriel nodded. "But not so very long ago this was part of Denmark."

Joshua the shepherd said they should hurry, and they crossed a landscape that became flatter and flatter the farther south they went. Between grazing land and enclosed pastures lay small villages, each with a little church and a few houses.

They were rushing through dense woodland when Joshua the shepherd stopped and knelt under a birch tree. He had found a sheep caught in a trap.

"The trap was probably set for a hare or a fox," he said.

He loosened a cord from the sheep's leg and added, "But now the sheep shall come with us to Bethlehem."

"Because it's one of us," said Ephiriel.

And the sheep seemed to answer. "Bah!" it bleated. "Baah."

Off they went: the lamb and the two sheep first, the shepherd behind them, Elisabet and Ephiriel last.

They entered a town and stopped in front of an old church with two tall towers over the entrance.

The angel told them that they were in Scania, that the town was called Lund, and that the big church was an ancient cathedral. He looked at his angel watch and said, "The watch says 1745. That proud cathedral has stood here for many, many centuries. Churches and cathedrals have been built all over the world, and it all started with the Christ Child who was born in Bethlehem. It's as if a tiny kernel of wheat is put into the ground and grows into a whole field full. The glory of heaven is very easily scattered about."

Elisabet wondered about what the angel had said. "Can we go in?" she asked.

The angel nodded, and they entered the great church. The sheep first, the shepherd next, and then Elisabet Hansen.

Inside, Elisabet heard the most beautiful sound. From the great organ there swelled such rich and powerful melodies that tears came to her eyes.

When the angel saw her, he said, "Yes, weep, my child. That wonderful music was composed by Johann Sebastian Bach. He is alive in Germany at this time, but his music will be heard throughout the world one day. That's not at all surprising, because his music is a tiny shred of the glory of heaven."

The only things that disturbed the music were two bleating sheep and a lamb scurrying about, so that its little bell tinkled.

A man in black robes came toward them from the chancel. It was the priest. "Get out, all of you!" he said sternly. "Lund Cathedral is not a common sheepfold."

Then the angel Ephiriel stepped in front of the priest. He spread out his wings and said, "The pastor should not be dismayed! He should remember that Jesus was born in a stable and that He was called the Good Shepherd."

The priest stopped abruptly, for even though he was a priest in an ancient cathedral, he was not really used to angels and the like.

He fell to his knees and folded his hands. "Glory to God in the highest!" he exclaimed.

They left him like that. The angel made a sign to the others that they should go. "Moments like that should never last too long," he said. "Perhaps he'll write a report to the bishop. Then the whole thing will be hushed up, or rumors will start to circulate about the miracle at Lund. In any case, the bishop should remind the pastor that the word 'pastor' means shepherd, neither more nor less."

Joshua struck his crook against the church wall. "To Bethlehem! To Bethlehem!"

They sped through a large park teeming with birds. A couple of soldiers came riding in their direction. When they saw the lively procession, they called out, "Halt!"

The men galloped toward them. But just as they bent down from their horses to seize Joshua the shepherd, they vanished like dew in sunshine.

Elisabet gaped, for the pilgrims were standing on the same spot as they had been before the soldiers rode up.

"They've disappeared!" she exclaimed.

The angel's laugh was like rippling water. "Yes, in a way. But we were the ones who disappeared. Perhaps they were so terrified when they saw what happened that they fell off their horses."

Elisabet was astonished, so Ephiriel had to explain to her again how they were traveling. "We're traveling in two directions at once. One journey goes south on the map to the town of Bethlehem in Judea. The other passes through history to David's city at the time when Jesus was born. It's a very unusual way of traveling; many people would say it was quite impossible, but nothing is impossible for God. For 'a thousand ages in thy sight are like an evening gone.' But the road to Bethlehem is exactly the same."

The angel's words astonished Elisabet and she hid them in her heart.

"It makes it simpler to avoid danger," remarked Joshua. "If we can't give the slip to severe priests or angry soldiers by taking a step to one side, we have to take a step back in time, instead. As little as fifteen minutes or half an hour can be sufficient."

With those words, they were on their way once more. They passed large fields and small villages. Soon they could glimpse the sea in the distance. In a short while, they were standing on a deserted beach.

"This is Øresund, the Sound," said Ephiriel. "My watch shows that 1703 years have passed since Jesus was born. We must get across to Denmark before the eighteenth century is over."

"Here's a rowboat," announced Joshua.

They climbed on board, the sheep first, Elisabet and Ephiriel behind them. Joshua pushed the boat out and jumped in at the last minute.

The angel Ephiriel rowed so hard that the spray foamed about the prow. The waves rocked the boat and the lamb's bell rang piercingly all the way across.

Joshua sat in the stern. Suddenly he said, "I can see Denmark."

☽ ☆

"I CAN see Denmark."

Joachim could almost see a little of Denmark, too, but it was only inside his head.

It was strange that Elisabet was able to travel back in time. And it was strange to think that two thousand years had passed since Jesus was born but the stories about Jesus had traveled through all those two thousand years, so that Joachim had heard about Him, too. Elisabet was traveling through time in the other direction.

When Mama and Papa got up, they came to see the picture in the Advent calendar. Joachim pointed to the boat with Elisabet, Ephiriel, Joshua, and the three sheep. But he said nothing about what had happened in the big park. He didn't tell them that the pilgrims had visited the cathedral in Lund, either. They would only have asked how he knew what a cathedral was, and Joachim had decided not to talk about the pieces of paper in the calendar.

After breakfast, they went into town to buy Christmas presents at the big department store. In the toy department on the first floor, Joachim started to think about Elisabet from the magic Advent calendar.

Could it have been from this store that she began running after the little lamb? There was an old escalator here. But wasn't it a very long time since Elisabet had chased the lamb?

"This shop must be forty years old," he said to his mother.

She looked at him oddly. "I should think it's even older than that" was all she said.

So he knew. Elisabet and the little lamb had run from this shop. He understood completely, because Joachim didn't like shopping in large stores, either. He got really angry at the nagging sound of the cash registers.

That Saturday was extra-long because he was thinking about what would happen when Elisabet and the angel Ephiriel got to Denmark. It was even worse at bedtime. He had to lie right under the magic calendar, which was still full to bursting with secrets.

To sleep so close to all those secrets was almost like living in a chocolate shop without being allowed to taste one single tiny chocolate.

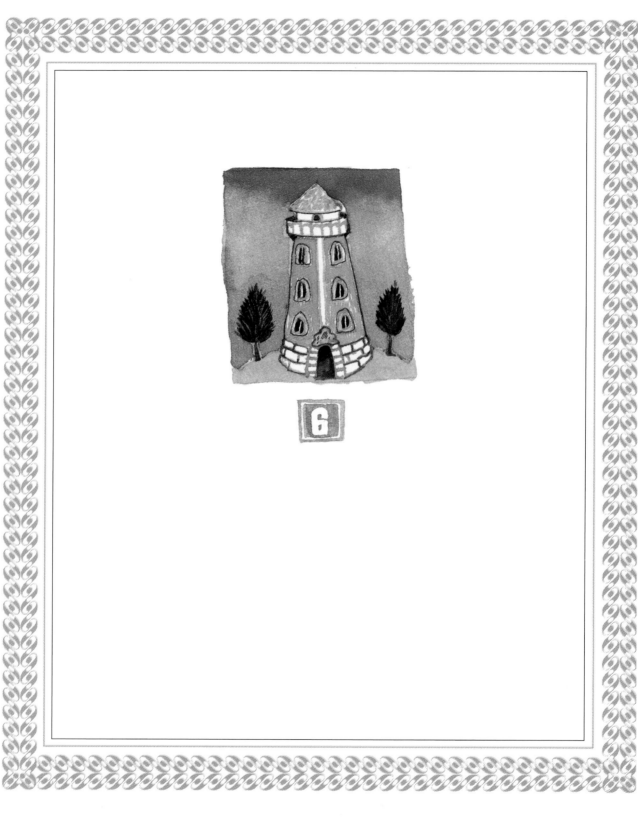

❧ DECEMBER 6 ❧

. . . a camel can move from
place to place as well, a little like the castles
on a chessboard . . .

WHEN Joachim woke up on Sunday morning, it felt as if he had just fallen asleep, for he hadn't woken once during the whole of that long night. Then he realized that he had dreamed, and as soon as he remembered the dream, it seemed to him that the night had been a long one, after all.

He had dreamed that the magic Advent calendar was filled with small chocolate figures that turned into real animals as soon as he opened the doors and let them out. To stop them from running away, he had to lock them up in his secret box, and he only let them out on Christmas Eve. Then all 24 chocolate animals crept out through the window and set off through the countryside. They were going to Bethlehem, to Bethlehem—because that's where the Christ Child was born. Joachim knew that Jesus had loved all of mankind, but in his dream he had liked chocolate as well.

Joachim sat up and laughed. He was ready to open the sixth door in the Advent calendar. Today there was a picture of a round tower. But he would look more closely at the picture afterwards. First he had to read what was on the piece of paper.

CASPAR

When the boat with Elisabet, the angel Ephiriel, Joshua the shepherd, and the three sheep touched land on the Danish side of Øresund, they were welcomed politely by a well-dressed man.

Elisabet spotted him first. The angel, who was rowing, sat with his back to the shore, and Joshua was busy keeping the sheep quiet.

"There's a man over there," she said.

The angel glanced over his shoulder and said, "Then he's one of us."

The man was black and was wearing a dark cloak with gold buttons, red knit pants, and sheepskin shoes. He came toward them and pulled the boat up on land. The sheep were the first to jump out, and soon the pilgrims were all standing on the beach.

The man wearing the fine clothes bent down and took Elisabet's hand. "Greetings to you, my child, and welcome to Sjaelland. My name is King Caspar of Nubia."

"Elisabet," said Elisabet, curtsying politely.

She wasn't quite sure how to behave. Perhaps she should have said that her name was Elisabet Hansen and that she came from Norway, but that wouldn't have been very interesting after he had told her that he was the King of Nubia.

"He's one of the Three Wise Men from the East," whispered Ephiriel solemnly.

"Or one of the Three Kings of the Orient," said Joshua, nodding.

None of this information made the situation any easier for Elisabet. If she was going to say anything, it would have to be that she was the Princess of Toten or something like that. Then maybe the King would have believed that Toten was a mighty kingdom.

The black king bowed again and said, "The pleasure is on my side of Øresund. You should know that I've been standing here waiting for you for so long that in the end I had to play hopscotch between 1701 and 1699."

This was so puzzling that Elisabet had to rub her eyes to see if she was awake. It was difficult enough to play hopscotch between squares on the pavement. How could the Wise Man play hopscotch between two different years?

He explained. "When I arrived on this shore in the Year of Our Lord 1701, some fishermen appeared, and they were so dismayed when they saw one of the Three Wise Men that I had to take a step back. That's how I got to the year 1700. I sat down and looked out over Øresund, but after a while a couple of soldiers on horseback came from the fortress in Copenhagen. They, too, were dismayed when they set eyes on a black king. You see, at the moment I am the only black man in the whole of Denmark, at least the only one who is a King of the Orient besides. That sort of thing attracts attention, my friends. People find it hard to become used to something completely different. So I hurried back to the year 1699, and since then I have been waiting here. I have seen neither man nor beast, and I have had no need to hide from sun and moon, or from the stars in heaven, either, for the stars in heaven are so close to God that they would never permit themselves to gossip about the life of humans on earth."

Elisabet didn't know whether she understood everything he said, but she did see that she was talking to a real wise man. He was so wise that she didn't know where to look.

So it was a great relief to her when at last the shepherd thumped his crook on the ground. "To Bethlehem! To Bethlehem!"

The little procession moved off again—the three sheep first, Joshua and Caspar the black king next, Elisabet and Ephiriel last.

They leapt along broad cobbled streets in a big city. Ephiriel explained that it was Copenhagen, the King's city. It was so early in the morning that the streets were almost deserted.

Elisabet thought it was nice to see such a big city without any cars. But you had to put up with the horse droppings that were fertilizing the streets. Elisabet was used to seeing that only when she visited her cousins at Toten.

"The time is 1648," announced the angel Ephiriel. "It's the last year of Christian IV's reign. He became King of Denmark and Norway when he was still a child, and that was many years ago."

"Of Norway, too?" asked Elisabet.

"Of Norway, too, yes. Because Norway is part of Denmark at this time. It was Christian IV who founded Kristiansand and Kongsberg. And he gave Oslo the name Christiania, too. He's very fond of Norway and has visited the country often."

They soon arrived at the very center of the Danish capital. They stopped in front of a church with a round tower at one end.

"That's the Round Tower which King Christian has just built onto the new Trinity Church," said Ephiriel. "Even though church towers look imposing, he thought they could be made better use of. So the Round Tower has been built both as a church tower and as a watchtower where astronomers can work in peace and quiet, studying the movements of the planets and the position of the stars in the sky. For these are the days when the first telescopes are being invented."

"That's a strange mixture," said Elisabet.

She felt that she, too, had to say something clever every now and again. But she had no luck this time, for the Wise Man shook his head. "The stars are created by God, too," he said. "So studying the stars in the sky can be like a whole church service. But here they have neither deserts nor camels."

Elisabet stared at him, and the Wise Man continued. "The best way to study the stars, in the opinion of all Wise Men, is to sit on the back of a camel in the desert. It's almost like sitting in a tower, but a camel can move from place to place as well, a little like the castles on a chessboard. The only thing that's a little difficult for a camel is to go through the eye of a needle."

Elisabet looked at the Wise Man in astonishment. She was not at all sure if she agreed that the back of a camel could be compared with a church tower. Nor was she so sure that a desert could be compared with a chessboard.

Caspar cleared his throat. "The drawback of a watchtower is that it usually stands stock-still. I have myself seen a tower that has stood in the same spot for more than a thousand years. The old walls must get bored with the view. On the other hand, they experience how people come and go, and perhaps that gives them insight."

Elisabet nodded, and with a gesture Caspar made sure that none of the others spoke. Then he eagerly continued.

"There are exactly two ways of becoming wise. One way is to travel out into the world and to see as much as possible of God's creation. The other is to put down roots in one spot and study everything that happens there in as much detail as you can. The problem is that it's totally impossible to do both at the same time."

Elisabet was again struck with wonder at the Wise Man's words. To be on the safe side, she clapped her hands, and the angel and the shepherd did the same. Caspar was infected by their enthusiasm and began clapping too, because he was so pleased with all that had been said.

Elisabet thought it must be fun to keep thinking thoughts that were so clever that people wanted to clap their hands.

It was as if the Wise Man had read her thoughts. He said, "Thinking clever thoughts is almost like being at a circus. And I don't mean a circus with clowns or elephants, but a real thinking circus. Let it be said once and for all, however: I am grateful to all clowns and elephants for their attention."

Joshua thumped his crook on the cobblestones. "To Bethlehem!" he said. "To Bethlehem!"

The procession began to move along the streets again: the sheep first, the shepherd, the Wise Man, the angel, and Elisabet following. Through the city and out to the country they went, between swaying wheat fields and cool, leafy woods. Elisabet thought Denmark was a very flat country. It seemed to be extra-flat, because she could see no tall buildings. The only things that pointed up occasionally were the churches they passed.

All of them had been built in honor of a little child who once upon a time was born in Bethlehem.

They saw the sea in the distance and came down to a small town called Korsør which lay beside the Great Belt, the broad sound between Sjaelland and Fyn.

The people in the small town almost fell over when they glimpsed the astonishing procession. But their terror lasted only a short time, for the next moment the procession had moved one or two weeks back in the history of the town. Then there were other people who glimpsed the pilgrimage for a second or two. That's why there was continual talk of angels at that time.

Joshua pointed to a large rowboat at the water's edge. "We have to borrow that," he said. "Hurry up, now. It's nearly 1600 years after Jesus' birth."

And he chased his sheep on board.

Elisabet felt she had to ask the angel whether this wasn't stealing, but Ephiriel reminded her that Jesus had to borrow an ass when he rode into Jerusalem.

A little later, they were out on the Great Belt. The angel rowed with one oar, King Caspar with the other. The Wise Man had to work hard to row as strongly as Ephiriel.

☽ ☆

WHEN Mama came in to look at the Advent calendar, Joachim forgot that he wasn't supposed to talk about what he had read.

She peered at the picture. "That must be the Tower of Babel."

Joachim shook his head. "Oh, no. That's the Round Tower in Copenhagen."

Mama looked at him in astonishment. "Who told you about that?"

"No idea," replied Joachim, because that's what Mama usually said when he asked her a question she couldn't answer. "Besides, it's impossible to play chess with a tower like that, because it stands stock-still. And if you sit in it you quickly get bored with the view. But, on the other hand, you may get some insight."

Mama clasped her hands. Joachim thought she did it because he had said something clever. But all she said was, "Oh, Joachim, where do you *get* all this from?"

❧ DECEMBER 7 ❧

. . . in heaven we've
always considered this to be
a slight exaggeration . . .

ALL that afternoon, Joachim thought about Caspar, the black king who had been waiting in Denmark for Elisabet, the angel Ephiriel, and Joshua the shepherd to come across Øresund.

How did he know they were coming? Did Ephiriel and the King of Nubia have an old agreement to meet precisely there in the year 1699? There was nothing to suggest that their meeting was accidental, after all. "Then he's one of us," the angel had said as soon as he saw Caspar.

It had all begun with the little lamb. Perhaps Elisabet hadn't been meant to follow it, but the angel in the woods must have known that the lamb would be coming that way?

All of a sudden, Joachim thought about the bookseller. He had said that the Advent calendar looked homemade, and Joachim agreed. It looked as if it had been cut out and glued at home in the kitchen.

If John had made the magic Advent calendar, he had probably named the girl in the story after Elisabet in the photograph. But why had he done that? Why had he made the Advent calendar and left it in a bookshop without knowing what would become of it?

In the evening, when Joachim was going to bed, he tried to push all the open doors shut so that he could look at the large picture. Before he put out the light, he glanced at the Advent calendar one more time, and thought how strange it must be to be in Bethlehem exactly at the time when Jesus was born.

Elisabet was on her way there, and, in a way, he was able to come along.

When he woke up the next morning, he opened the seventh door and saw a picture of a sheep eating grass in front of some high walls.

THE FOURTH SHEEP

The angel Ephiriel and King Caspar had rowed Elisabet, Joshua the shepherd, and the three sheep over the Great Belt.

"We're going ashore again," said Ephiriel. "This island is called Fyn, and it's exactly 1599 years since Jesus was born in Bethlehem."

From the sea they ran toward a large castle on a mound between ramparts and moats. "That's Nyborg Castle," the angel told them. "We're standing in front of the oldest royal fortress in Scandinavia."

Elisabet pointed up at the ramparts. "There's a sheep."

The angel nodded. "Then it's one of us."

With that, they all leaped up onto the ramparts, the three sheep first, Joshua and King Caspar after them, Elisabet and Ephiriel last.

A soldier rushed out from between the buildings of the castle. He raised a spear and shouted, "Sheep thieves!"

The next moment, three or four soldiers came storming up. All of them had spears, and one of them had a kind of gun as well. The angel Ephiriel stepped forward. The soldiers threw themselves down on the ground and hid their heads in their hands.

"Fear not!" said the angel in a gentle voice. "For I bring you tidings of great joy. This sheep will come with us to the Holy Land where the Christ Child is to be born."

Only one of the soldiers dared to look up. He was the one who had called them sheep thieves. "Be merciful unto us and take the sheep with you," he cried.

The sheep had already joined the others as if it belonged to the little flock. Joshua struck his crook against the rampart and said, "To Bethlehem! To Bethlehem!"

Off they went across the green island, the four sheep first, Joshua, Caspar, Ephiriel, and Elisabet following them.

On the bank of a small river they passed a town with narrow streets and one-story dwellings. On the outskirts stood an ancient stone church with a square tower.

"That's the great cathedral of Odense," said Ephiriel. "It's named after Saint Canute, who was killed here in the year 1086."

Elisabet pointed at Ephiriel's arm. The gold and mother-of-pearl was glittering.

"What time is it on your angel watch?"

"It's 1537 years after Christ. From now on, the Bible will be printed in all the languages of the world, so everyone can read about Jesus, for in these days the art of printing will be invented. Before this, books have had to be written by hand, and only the priests were able to read the Bible.

But not many people have learned to read. Now it is decided that all the nation must go to school."

"Some years before this time," Caspar said, "a Polish astronomer called Copernicus appeared. He insisted that the earth was as round as a ball and moves in orbit round the sun. This wasn't news to wise men, but to most people it was a strange and exciting idea. Sailors could now travel around the world, and that's how Christopher Columbus reached America in the year 1492. Then the Spanish sailors attacked the Indians cruelly. In the opinion of the Kings of the Orient, it would have been better if they had kept to the ships of the desert. For there is no more peaceful animal than a camel in the desert, and peace is the message of Christmas."

Elisabet understood about half of what the Wise Man said when Joshua struck the ground with his crook. "To Bethlehem! To Bethlehem!"

They went on their way along a ridge that gave them a good view over Fyn. Now and then, they looked down on a horse drawing a plow or an ox harnessed to a cart.

"It's not so flat here," said Elisabet as she ran. "But we're still in Denmark, aren't we?"

The angel nodded. "Yes indeed, and the Danes are very proud of ridges like this. But we're no more than a hundred meters above sea level. They have called the hillsides we can see down there on the left the Fyn Alps. Another ridge is called Himmel, Heavenly, Mountain. In heaven we've always considered this to be a slight exaggeration."

The procession had paused, and Caspar joined in the conversation again. "But it's important to be happy with what you have. However little it is, it's infinitely more than nothing."

Elisabet stood still and thought seriously before she said, "If the world was as smooth as a ball, there wouldn't be a single mountain on the whole earth. But then even a rocky slope would be just as exciting as the highest mountain in Norway, as long as it was the only rocky slope."

"So you see," said Caspar, nodding.

Elisabet didn't quite understand what he meant.

"So you see how easily clever ideas travel," continued the Wise Man. "You've been with a Wise Man for only a short time, but you've already understood a tiny part of the heavenly wisdom. Bravo!"

Elisabet was glad she had said something clever. She felt so encouraged that she tried again. "And if the world was as small as the moon, nobody would complain that it hadn't been made a little bit larger."

Caspar put his hand on her head. "How true that is. Even if the world had been no larger than a pea, it would have been just as big a mystery. For where would the little pea have come from? That, too, would have had to be created by God. And it's no easier to create a pea than to create a whole solar system."

Elisabet thought the last statement a slight exaggeration. For if the world hadn't been any larger than a pea, it wouldn't have had room even for Adam and Eve.

It was as if the Wise Man was afraid she was going to protest. He quickly continued. "Even if there had been only one star in the sky, that one star would have aroused just as much wonder as all the other stars together. After all, nobody goes around complaining because there's only one moon. On the contrary: if there had been a hundred moons, they would only have gotten in each other's way. So the creation of billions of stars in the sky was a luxurious exaggeration. Whenever there's too much of anything, you can stare at it without appreciating it. That's how it's possible to be out under a starry sky and fail to see a single star because of a shower of shooting stars."

It was quite true, thought Elisabet. She had often looked at a sky full of stars without noticing any particular one.

Caspar continued. "In the opinion of the Kings of the Orient, God spoiled humans a little, because He created far too much at the same time. He created so many strange things to look at that many people don't see God. But that's how He managed to hide Himself, too. He wouldn't have been able to do that if only four people, three trees, two sheep, and eight camels existed in the whole of creation. If only one fish could be found in the sea, people would probably have noticed how perfect it was. And then they might have started asking who had made it."

For a while he stood there looking around him. Elisabet thought he was waiting for someone to clap. To be on the safe side, she clapped. Then the others clapped as well.

"There, there," said Caspar. "That wasn't so much to clap for."

Then he seemed to change his mind. "Although it was infinitely more than nothing."

The procession of pilgrims ran down toward a little town beside a narrow strip of water.

"This sound is called the Little Belt, and the name of the little town is Middelfart," said Ephiriel. "The time is 1504 years after Christ."

Before Elisabet was able to ask how they were going to cross the sound, Joshua was on his way toward a boat that lay moored to a little pier. In the boat sat a young man drawing up a fishing line. When he saw the angel Ephiriel, he dropped the line into the sea and threw himself down with his head on the deck.

"Be not afraid," said Ephiriel. "We are pilgrims on our way to the Holy Land, where Jesus is to be born. Can you row us over the Little Belt?"

"Amen," replied the ferryman. "Amen, amen . . ."

The angel knew his answer meant yes. The four sheep and the rest of the pilgrims climbed on board the boat.

As the ferryman rowed across the sound, he stared and stared at the angel Ephiriel. It was probably the first time he had seen a proper angel. He didn't so much as glance at the black king, Caspar.

If the angel had not been with them, Elisabet thought, the ferryman would most certainly have had more than enough to do, staring at King Caspar, since it was also probably the first time he had seen a black man. Only if the King had not been with them either, would he perhaps have looked at her. She thought it was a little unfair that the world should be like that.

When they reached the other side and the sheep began jumping out of the boat, they said thank you and goodbye to the ferryman. As for the ferryman, he only repeated what he had said many, many times already. "Amen, amen . . ."

☽ ☆

JOACHIM had just finished reading when Mama came into the room. He crumpled up the thin paper quickly, but Mama saw that he was hiding something.

"What are you holding in your hand?"

"Nothing," he said. "Only air."

"May I see it, then?"

But Joachim held the crumpled paper so hard that his knuckles went white.

"It's a Christmas present," he said.

The words "Christmas present" might have been magic. At any rate, they made Mama smile. "For me?"

Joachim nodded.

"Then I won't look," said Mama. "But it must be a very tiny Christmas present."

"It's infinitely bigger than nothing," said Joachim.

Joachim thought it was strange that everything that had to do with Christmas was so special. It was one of the most secret things in the whole world.

But Mama was wrong about one thing. What he was holding in his hand wasn't such a tiny Christmas present.

8

❊ DECEMBER 8 ❊

. . . part of the glory
of heaven that has strayed
down to earth . . .

O N December 8, Joachim was woken by Mama. She ruffled his hair and said, "Time to get up, Joachim. It's half past seven, and you start school early today."

He sat up in bed. The first thing he thought of was the magic Advent calendar hanging above his head.

Mama seemed to read his mind. "But you have time to open the Advent calendar."

Joachim thought quickly. He thought so quickly that there was room for an awful lot of thoughts before Mama went on. "Aren't you going to open it? I'd like to see it, too."

No! thought Joachim.

He *couldn't* open the magic Advent calendar while Mama was watching.

"I don't think you're quite awake yet," Mama said. "Perhaps you'll let me open the Advent calendar today?"

"No!" said Joachim, so loud and clear that Mama jumped. "I'll wait till I come home from school. Because . . . I'll have more time then."

He jumped out of bed quickly to be certain Mama wasn't going to open the calendar.

"Of course you do whatever you want," she said.

She went out to the kitchen while Joachim got dressed.

☽ ☆

WHEN he came home from school, a man was standing outside the garden gate. Since he didn't know the man, Joachim pretended he hadn't seen him. He opened the gate and closed it after him. Then the stranger walked toward him.

"Is your name Joachim?" he asked.

Joachim stopped on the path that Papa had almost cleared of snow, and turned toward the man. He was very old; he looked very kind, too. All the same, Joachim didn't like someone he didn't know to know his name. But he had to answer.

"Yes," he said. "That's me."

The man nodded. He came right up to the gate. He was wearing a green felt hat.

"I thought so."

He had an odd accent. Perhaps he wasn't Norwegian. "You've received a fine Advent calendar, haven't you?"

Joachim gave a start. How did the man know that?

"A magic Advent calendar," Joachim said.

"A magic Advent calendar, yes. Price: 75 øre. My name's John. I sell flowers at the market."

Joachim stood still. In his Advent calendar he had read about people who had suddenly seen an angel. Now it was almost as if he was being visited by an angel himself.

He knew this meeting with the flower seller was important and he wanted to say something serious, but he only managed, "How did you know where I lived?"

John chuckled. "Good question, my boy," he said. "I often go into the book-shop, you see. I like it there. So I wanted to hear where the old calendar had ended up. It was a good thing your father forgot his driver's license. If he hadn't, it would have been much more difficult for me to find you. But I expect you'd have come to see me at the market sooner or later. Don't you think?"

Joachim nodded. He *had* thought of it. "Did you know there were some mysterious pieces of paper in the Advent calendar?" he asked.

The old man smiled with an air of secrecy. "If there's anyone in the whole world who does know, it must be me. Now you know, too."

"Is it homemade?"

"Completely homemade, yes, and very old. But that's an old story, too. Have you opened the calendar today?"

Joachim shook his head. "I have to do it when Mama and Papa aren't looking, because I don't want them to know about the pieces of paper. I'm going to wrap them up on Christmas Eve and put the package under the Christmas tree for them."

"That's a good idea," said John. "But what about yesterday? Did the pilgrims take a sheep with them from the old castle on Fyn, and did the angel Ephiriel say 'Fear not' to the sentries at the castle?"

Joachim was almost scared, because John knew all about it. "Did *you* make the magic Advent calendar?" he asked.

"Yes and no . . ."

Joachim was afraid John might leave, so he quickly asked another question. "Has it all really happened, or have you made it up?"

John looked serious. "It's all right to ask . . . but it isn't always so easy to answer."

Joachim said, "I wondered if Elisabet in the magic Advent calendar is the same as the Elisabet whose picture was in the bookstore."

"So he told you about the old picture?" said John, sighing. "Well, I have nothing to hide anymore, I'm too old for that now. But it isn't Christmas yet, so we'd better talk about Elisabet another time."

He took a step back. "Sabet . . . Tebas . . ." he mumbled to himself. Joachim didn't understand, but perhaps he hadn't been meant to hear.

Finally John said, "I must go now. But we'll meet again, for that old story links us human beings together." He walked away at a brisk pace.

Joachim was annoyed that he hadn't had time to ask more questions. He definitely should have asked whether the big calendar picture was gradually changing as he read the pieces of paper.

He hurried into the house and opened the calendar door with the number 8 on it. Today there was a picture of a shepherd carrying a lamb on his shoulders.

JACOB

On one of the last days of the year 1499 after Christ, four sheep, one shepherd, one King of the Orient, one angel, and a little girl from Norway jumped out of a boat that had brought them across the Little Belt to Jutland.

"Thank goodness!" exclaimed Caspar as they stepped on land.

"Yes, it'll be a long time before we have to do that again," said Joshua.

The angel Ephiriel nodded. "Verily I say unto you that we will cross the sea only one more time before we get to Bethlehem."

Elisabet had no idea what they were talking about.

"Isn't it still terribly far to Bethlehem?" she asked.

"Yes, indeed," said the angel. "It is far, and many hundreds of years, too. But we have only one more sea to cross. That won't happen until we get to the Black Sea."

They came to a town on the inland end of a fjord. At one end of the town was a large fortress.

"This town is called Kolding and is in South Jutland," said the angel Ephiriel. "It has been an important trading center for hundreds of years. The fortress is called Koldinghus and the kings of Denmark have often lived here. The time is 1488 years after Christ's birth."

Joshua struck the ground with his crook. "To Bethlehem! To Bethlehem!"

They came to the top of a ridge with a fine view over the countryside. Flowers grew everywhere, so it must be early summer.

Elisabet pointed down as she ran. "Look at the lovely wildflowers!" she said.

The angel nodded mysteriously. "They are part of the glory of heaven that has strayed down to earth," he explained. "You see, there's so much glory in heaven that it's very easy for it to spill over."

Elisabet pondered the angel's words and hid them in her heart.

Suddenly the shepherd stopped and pointed at the little flock of sheep. "A lamb is missing!"

He needed to say no more, for they all saw that the earth had seemingly swallowed up the little lamb with the bell.

"Where is it?" asked Elisabet.

Joshua shook his head. "Usually they're so sweet and their fleece is so white that they're a delight to the eye, but they're also so wild that they're almost uncontrollable. It doesn't always help to put a bell on them. If I'm watching one lamb, the other will suddenly vanish. And when I find the second lamb, all of a sudden the first lamb will decide to leave the flock. Shepherding is a difficult job, and it's especially difficult to herd sheep all the way to Bethlehem. As it is written, now I must leave the other sheep to look for the one lamb that is missing."

Elisabet felt her eyes fill with tears. But just then a man appeared over the crest of the ridge. He was wearing clothes exactly like Joshua's. On his shoulders he was carrying the lamb with the bell.

"He is one of us," said Ephiriel.

The man put the lamb down at Elisabet's feet. He held out his hand to Joshua and said, "I am Jacob the shepherd and the second of the shepherds in the field. Now I'll help to care for the flock that's going to Bethlehem."

Elisabet clapped her hands. Joshua struck the ground with his crook and said, "To Bethlehem! To Bethlehem!"

As they passed the old market town of Flensburg, the angel Ephiriel said, "The time is 1402 after the birth of Christ. We shall soon be crossing the border into Germany and diving into the depths of the Middle Ages."

☽ ☆

JOACHIM stood lost in thought. The angel Ephiriel had said that the wildflowers were a part of the glory of heaven that had strayed down to earth.

Because there's so much glory in heaven that it's easy for it to spill over. Probably only a flower seller could write something like that.

He didn't tell Mama and Papa that John had visited him. If he told them about that, he would have to give away the secret of the scraps of paper, too.

Joachim now had so many secrets to keep that his head might split at any moment.

. . . they had broken a solemn promise . . .

NOW Joachim had met John, the old flower seller. John knew more about the Advent calendar than he wanted to share. He had said he would tell Joachim more about Elisabet another time, because it was not Christmas yet.

But what had he muttered to himself?

Joachim couldn't stop thinking about it for the rest of the afternoon. "Sabet . . . Tebas."

Who or what was Sabet and Tebas? Could those strange words have anything to do with the magic Advent calendar?

Before he went to bed he wrote the words down in a little notebook so as not to forget them by morning. Then he discovered something odd: SABET became TEBAS when he read it backward. So of course TEBAS turned into SABET, too.

This was so mysterious that he wrote down the two words like this:

<pre>
        S
        A
T E B A S
        E
        T
</pre>

Perhaps one day the magic words would help him to understand the old Advent calendar.

Suddenly he remembered something the bookseller had said. Hadn't he said that the old flower seller was a little odd? Joachim didn't think he seemed the least bit odd. Of course, it was unusual to pour water over people's heads, but it was just the sort of thing that Joachim might suddenly decide to do himself.

☽ ☆

WHEN he woke up on the ninth of December, he quickly opened the Advent calendar before Mama and Papa woke up and came into his room. It was a picture of a man playing a pipe. After the man came a long procession of children, some big and some small.

THE FIFTH SHEEP

It was the year 1378 after Christ. Three godly sheep and a lamb with a bell stormed into the city of Hamburg. Behind the little flock ran two shepherds in light blue tunics. One of them was carrying the kind of shepherd's crook you often see in southern countries. An elegantly dressed black king followed the shepherds. Behind the King, a little girl was running as fast as her short legs would carry her. After the girl, an angel hovered just above the ground.

It was Sunday and early in the morning. A few people were on their way to morning Mass in the old Church of St. Jacobi. As soon as they saw the procession of pilgrims, they began gesturing with their arms. Some of them shaded their eyes, and one of them exclaimed, "God be praised!"

Something similar had happened in the town of Hanover a few years earlier. It was 1351, immediately after the fearful Plague that had cost so many human lives, not only in Germany but in all of Europe. It was a Monday, and the stands on the great market square were about to open. Peasants in their worn homespun clothes and market women in coarse skirts had begun setting out their wares. All of them had lost some of their dear ones. It was just before the dawn of a new day.

It was then that a little flock of sheep suddenly ran into the market. One of the sheep overturned a table of vegetables. After the sheep there came a strange group. There were a couple of shepherds, and a black man in exotic clothes. The black man was followed by a white-clad figure with wings on its back. At the very end came a little girl. She stumbled over the shaft of a cart full of cabbages and lay there after the rest of the godly company had left the market.

Elisabet wept bitterly when she saw the angel Ephiriel and all the others disappearing. It was the second time on the long journey south that she had fallen and hurt herself. The first time, she had lost the lamb. Now she had lost the procession of pilgrims and was surrounded by people she didn't know. Not only was she in a foreign country; she was in a foreign century, too.

The people in the market were terrified by what they had seen. They crowded around Elisabet, and a man poked her with his foot as if he was afraid to touch her. He wrinkled his nose and grunted horribly. But soon an old woman helped Elisabet back on her feet and tried to comfort her. She spoke a language Elisabet didn't understand.

"I'm going to Bethlehem," said Elisabet.

And the market woman replied, "Hamelin? Hamelin?"

"No, no!" Elisabet said, sobbing. "To Bethlehem! To Bethlehem!"

Those were her words. The next moment, one of the angels of the Lord appeared in an arc of light above the market. Elisabet stretched out her arms toward the angel and cried, "Ephiriel! Ephiriel!"

The people in the market threw themselves down to the ground, but the angel lifted Elisabet into the air, flew over the spire of the new Market Church, and was gone.

He put her down on a country road outside the town. There the sheep, the shepherds, and King Caspar were waiting. The three men clapped their hands.

"Isn't that just what I was saying?" Joshua said, chuckling. "When one of the lambs is lost, the shepherd must leave his flock and find the lamb that has wandered away."

He struck the ground with his crook. "To Bethlehem! To Bethlehem!"

"How far is it to Bethlehem?" asked Elisabet.

"Not very far, my dear," said Ephiriel.

After a while, they came to a town on the bank of another river.

"This is Hamelin," said Ephiriel. "The river is called the Weser, and the year is 1304 after Jesus' birth. A few years ago, a dreadful misfortune occurred in this town. Well . . . in a way, they had only themselves to blame. For they had broken a solemn promise, and that's something one should never do."

"What happened?" asked Elisabet.

"The town had been plagued by rats for a long time. But then a rat catcher arrived in town. He played on a magic pipe, and the sound of the pipe made all the rats follow him. That way, the piper led the rats to the river, where they all drowned."

"Wasn't that a good thing?"

"Yes, of course, but the people in the town had promised the man a big reward if he could save them from the plague of rats. When he got rid of the rats, they refused to pay what they owed him."

"What did the rat catcher do then?"

"He began to play on his magic pipe again, and now it was all the children in the town who were bewitched by the music of the pipe and followed him. They disappeared inside a huge mountain, together with the piper, and were never seen again."

Elisabet realized that the woman in the market at Hanover had probably thought she was one of the children who had been lured into the mountain by the rat catcher from Hamelin.

They were about to hurry on through Europe and even further back into history, when a sheep came running toward them along the road and joined the other sheep. Now the flock numbered five.

Joshua struck the ground with his crook. "To Bethlehem! To Bethlehem!"

꒷ ☆

JOACHIM found the key to his box and hid the thin piece of paper. When Mama came in a little later, he was sitting looking at the picture in the Advent calendar.

Mama leaned over him. "Well, look at that. A piper . . ."

"He's a rat catcher," said Joachim. "They wouldn't give him his reward for taking all the rats away from Hamelin, so he took all the children away with him, instead. The people in the town had broken a solemn promise, and that's something one should never do."

Then Papa came in. "What are you two talking about?" he asked.

Only then did Joachim realize that he had forgotten again to be silent about what he had read on the piece of paper.

"I'm making it up," he said. "It's something I'm inventing."

"No, it isn't, Joachim," said Papa firmly. "You were talking about the Pied Piper of Hamelin, and that's an old story from Germany. Who has told you about that?"

What could he say? He had to come up with something clever. "Ingvild," he said. She was his teacher. "Or maybe it was someone in the class."

He was lying. But wasn't he allowed to lie about a Christmas present? Wasn't that the only thing in the whole world that you could lie about as much as you liked?

After school, Mama and Joachim went into town to do some shopping. On the way home, Joachim asked whether they could stop by the market square.

There were not as many people in the market as in summer. Some stands sold wreaths and candles; others sold all kinds of crafts.

"I wonder how they can stand here in the middle of winter," said Mama, shivering. "There's even someone over there selling flowers."

Joachim laughed inside. "That's because part of the glory of heaven strayed down to earth," he said.

Mama pulled on his hand. "What *are* you talking about?" she said.

"He's selling flowers in the middle of the winter because the glory of heaven has strayed down to earth," repeated Joachim. "You see, there's so much glory in heaven that it's easy for it to spill over."

Mama shook her head and sighed. Obviously, she didn't like him using so many unusual words.

John was standing behind a table with lots of flowers on it. He winked at Joachim and waved discreetly.

After they passed, Joachim turned around. John was pretending to play on an invisible pipe.

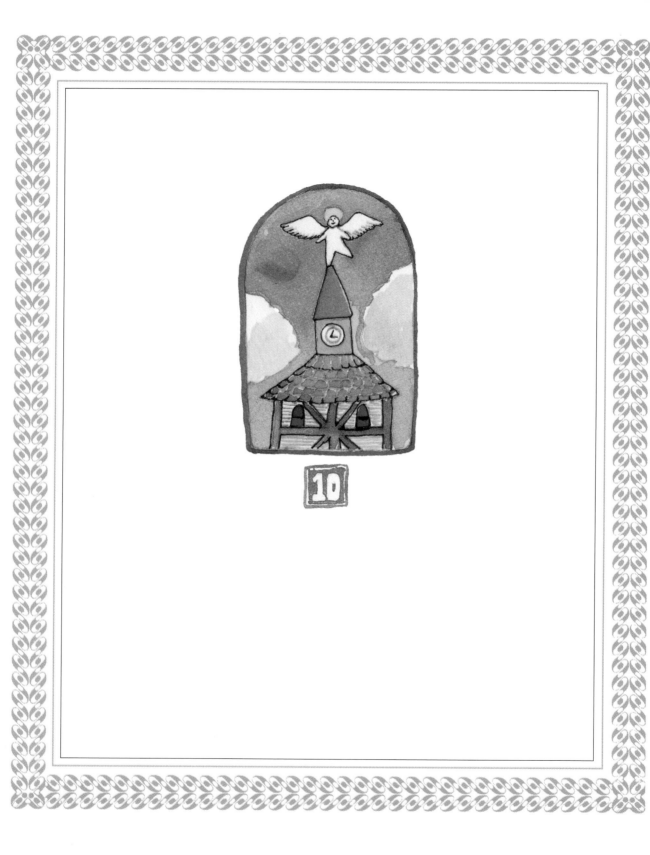

❖ DECEMBER 10 ❖

. . . a few seconds later, what Elisabet
had thought was a bird took off and flew down
in a spiral toward the pilgrims . . .

JOACHIM woke up the next day and opened the tenth door in the magic Advent calendar. Today there was a picture of an angel at the top of a church tower.

IMPURIEL

It happened at Paderborn at the end of the thirteenth century. Into the little town halfway between Hanover and Cologne rushed a frisky flock of sheep, followed by two shepherds, a black king, a little girl in a red jacket and blue pants, and an angel with outspread wings.

It was early in the morning; only a night watchman was out in the streets. He called out sternly to the two shepherds, who were chasing their flock of sheep through the town. The next moment, he saw the angel hovering above the cobblestones. Then he raised his arms to the sunrise and exclaimed, "Hallelujah! Hallelujah!"

Whereupon he retreated around a corner, leaving the streets to the godly procession.

They stopped in front of a church in the middle of the town.

"That's St. Bartholomew's Church," said Ephiriel. "It was built in the eleventh century and is named after one of Jesus' twelve apostles. It is said of Bartholomew that he journeyed all the way to India to tell the people there about Jesus."

Elisabet had noticed something strange. She pointed up at the spire on the church tower. "There's a white bird sitting up there," she said.

Ephiriel smiled. "If only there were." He sighed.

A few seconds later, what Elisabet had thought was a bird took off and flew down in a spiral toward the pilgrims. Long before it landed, Elisabet realized that it wasn't a bird at all but an angel. But it was not a grown angel; it was no larger than she was herself.

The child angel alighted right in front of Elisabet's feet. "Hi!" he exclaimed. "My name is Impuriel and I'm coming with you to Bethlehem."

He whirled around a little, peered up at Caspar and the two shepherds, and behaved very frivolously. Finally, he looked up at Ephiriel and said, "I've been waiting for a quarter of an eternity."

Caspar cleared his throat firmly. It was obvious he had something on his mind.

"A quarter of an eternity," he began. "That's about 66,289 years . . . or about 156,498 years . . . or, more exactly, 439,811,977 years . . . or perhaps even a little more. It's not easy to say exactly how long a quarter of an eternity lasts. First you have to find out how long a *whole* eternity lasts, then you have to divide it by four, but exactly how long a whole eternity lasts is very difficult to calculate. No matter which number you start with, eternity will in fact last even longer. So one can say that a quarter of an eternity is exactly as long as a whole eternity. Even a thousandth of an eternity is precisely just as long as the whole of the rest of eternity. This is extremely difficult to understand, for calculating whole or half or quarter eternities is a matter for heaven alone."

The cherub Impuriel looked offended. "In any case, I've been sitting on top of the church tower for *hours*," he said.

"Very possibly, but that's not the same as sitting there for a quarter of an eternity," said Caspar.

To avoid a quarrel between the Wise Man and the cherub, and not just a quarter of a quarrel, Joshua struck the cobblestones with his crook, saying, "To Bethlehem! To Bethlehem!"

They set off through the town and out along the roads and cattle trails. Impuriel leaped in front of the five sheep. So the pilgrims were guarded by angels at both ends.

They saw many towns and villages, but didn't stop until they came to the old Roman colonial city of Cologne on the bank of the Rhine River. Ephiriel had explained that their route through Europe had been planned so they would be seen by as few people as possible.

"Angel time says it's 1272 years after Christ," he said, pointing up at a big cathedral that was being built. "They've started to build the great Cathedral of Cologne, but it won't be finished for many hundreds of years."

Joshua banged with his crook. "To Bethlehem! To Bethlehem!"

Impuriel turned around and said, "Wonderful countryside, isn't it? We're going up the marvelous Rhine Valley. There are fortresses and castles, steep vineyards and Gothic cathedrals, dandelions and rhubarb."

They hurried along the bank of the biggest river Elisabet had ever seen. The valley became narrower and narrower and the mountains higher and higher. They ran past small towns and villages. Out on the river floated an occasional barge.

As they sped through the beautiful landscape, Elisabet turned toward Ephiriel and asked whether he had met Impuriel before.

The angel thought her question was so funny he couldn't help laughing. "All the angels in heaven have known each other through all eternity," he said.

"Are there a lot of you?"

"Yes, a whole host."

"How can you all know each other, then?"

"We've had all eternity to get to know each other, and that's a very long time."

Elisabet had to think hard to understand what Ephiriel meant.

The angel went on. "If you have a party that lasts for three hours, you shouldn't invite more than five or six guests, so that everyone will be able to talk to everyone else. But if the party lasts for three whole days, you can easily have fifty or more guests."

Elisabet nodded. She had discussed this with Mama every year about her birthday.

Ephiriel spread his arms. "The heavenly party has lasted for all eternity."

Elisabet wanted to know more. "Do all the angels have different names?"

"Of course. Otherwise we couldn't address each other. Otherwise, we wouldn't have been people, either."

And Ephiriel began to recite all the angels' names, one by one.

"The angels in heaven are called Ariel, Beriel, Curruciel, Daniel, Ephiriel, Fabiel, Gabriel, Hammarubiel, Impuriel, Joachiel, Kachaduriel, Luxuriel, Michael, Narriel . . ."

"That's enough," said Elisabet. "How long would you have to go on talking to name *all* the angels?"

"I would have had to go on for all eternity."

Elisabet shook her head. "That's pretty good going, to remember all the names by heart."

"With all eternity at your disposal, it's not so difficult."

Elisabet felt dizzy, but she wasn't going to give up. "Anyway, I think it's very clever to think up so many different names all ending in -el."

Ephiriel nodded. "God's imagination is just as infinite as there are infinitely many stars in the sky. No angel is exactly like another, nor are humans, either. You can make a thousand identical machines, but they are so easy to make that even a human can do it."

Finally, the angel Ephiriel said something that Elisabet hid in her heart. "Every person on earth is a unique work of creation."

꒱ ☆

JOACHIM smiled to himself. It had been so much fun to read about all the angels. Suddenly he heard Mama on the landing. He slid the paper under his pillow.

Mama leaned over the bed to peep in the calendar. "An angel," she said, "on a church tower."

And then something stupid happened. Again Joachim forgot that he wasn't supposed to talk about what he had read. Perhaps it was because he was trying to remember all those strange angel names. He said, "That's the cherub Impuriel."

Mama stared at him. "Impuriel?"

Joachim nodded. He thought it was a nice name for a mischievous angel. "He's sitting on the top of St. Bartholomew's Church. He's been sitting there for a quarter of an eternity, but now he's about to take off and fly in a spiral down to Elisabet and the others."

Mama didn't say anything to Joachim. Instead, she called Papa. When he came into the room, she asked Joachim to tell him what the church in the picture was called.

Oh, no! Only then did Joachim realize that he had said too much.

"St. Bartholomew's Church," he said. "Bartholomew went all the way to India and told the people there about Jesus. But the church is in Germany, in Paderburg, or something like that."

Mama and Papa looked at each other.

"I'll check it in the encyclopedia," said Papa. "Then we'll find out."

When he came back, he looked as if he had met an angel or two on the landing. "He's right. The town's called Paderborn, and there really is an old St. Bartholomew's Church there."

They were staring at Joachim just as they had done the time he ate nearly all the Christmas cookies the day before Christmas Eve.

Papa took the magic Advent calendar down from the wall and inspected it on both sides. Then he hung it up again.

"And how did you hear about Bartholomew?" asked Papa. "Or about Paderborn, for that matter?"

"At school," said Joachim.

"Is that the truth?"

Either you were allowed to tell lies about Christmas presents or you weren't.

"Yes," whispered Joachim.

By then, it was so late that there was no more time to discuss Bartholomew, Impuriel, or Paderborn. Neither Mama nor Papa had time to make their sandwiches for lunch.

Joachim's most important victory that morning was that he managed to hide the thin piece of paper in his secret box before he ran off to school. He hid the key in the bookshelf.

When he came home from school, Mama was there. She had opened his secret box!

She had opened his secret box. Mama had done something she had promised she would never do. She had broken a solemn promise. She had done something that was just as bad as opening other people's letters.

On the dining table lay the ten sheets of thin paper that Joachim had found in the magic Advent calendar.

He was furious. He was so angry with Mama that he felt like hitting her.

"You *promised* me that the secret box was *mine* and that you'd *never* open it," he said. "So you tell lies. And you steal, too."

Then Papa came home. He had talked to Mama on the phone. It was he who had said she should find the key and open the secret box. They had to find out how Joachim knew so many strange names and used so many grownup words.

Joachim said they shouldn't have been allowed to have children. People who tell lies to their children might suddenly hit them as well, he said—and that was against the law. They could at least have waited until he came home from school and asked if they could open his box. Finally, he managed to say that he had hidden all the mysterious scraps of paper because he wanted to wrap them up and give them to Mama and Papa for Christmas. He said he'd throw away the magic Advent calendar. Then he began to cry. He ran into his room and slammed the door as hard as he could.

He was never going to forgive them! He would never listen to them again, either. He would never believe anything they said. Never!

Joachim sat on his bed and looked up at the magic Advent calendar, but his eyes were so full of tears that the colors slid into one another and he could not pick out the angels from the shepherds in the fields. Everything was ruined. The Advent calendar had become ordinary, like every other Advent calendar. It wasn't the least bit magical anymore.

After a long time, something began to sing in his ears, and the song he heard was: SABET—TEBAS—SABET—TEBAS—SABET—TEBAS . . .

It was such a mysterious song that he began to realize that it didn't make any difference whether Mama and Papa knew about the scraps of paper in the Advent calendar. Perhaps the magic Advent calendar was so full of secrets that there would be enough for the whole family.

He had still not told them that he had met John. That was something he had kept to himself.

There was a knock at the door. Joachim didn't answer, but after a little while Papa opened the door cautiously. "It's true, we did something stupid," he said.

Then Mama came up. "Can you forgive us?" she said.

Joachim stared at the floor. "Maybe . . ."

Nobody said anything.

"Did you read what was on the papers?" asked Joachim.

"I suppose I did," Mama said. "But, you see, I don't know which piece of paper came out of the calendar first. Maybe you can show us—maybe you'd read it to Papa?"

Joachim considered carefully. "Well, all right."

In a way, he was a little relieved. From now on, he had no need to hide anything. Besides, he would be able to ask Mama and Papa if he read something he didn't understand.

From now on, the magic Advent calendar would be the whole family's Advent calendar.

11

❊ DECEMBER 11 ❊

. . . many people are terribly
frightened when they see one of the
angels of the Lord . . .

THE rest of the afternoon was spent poring over the scraps of paper that had fallen out of the magic Advent calendar. Joachim put them in the right order, so that Mama and Papa could read the story.

As they read, Papa said, "That's the strangest thing I've ever heard. I wonder how many calendars like this were made . . ."

And Mama kept saying, "I've never seen anything like it . . . Imagine bringing home *this* Advent calendar, Joachim!"

When it was evening and Joachim had to go to bed, he sat up for a long time staring at the magic Advent calendar. And it happened again.

It happened again! On the big calendar picture, there were many angels hovering in the sky. Joachim had seen that before. But today he discovered that one of the angels was a cherub.

He was quite sure. Impuriel had not been in the picture until Joachim had read that he flew in spirals down from the tall church tower.

"Mama!" he shouted. "Papa!"

Both of them came rushing into his room. They were obviously afraid that something dreadful had happened to him. He *was* a bit shocked himself.

"I can see the angel Impuriel!" was all he said.

Mama and Papa turned. Perhaps they thought he had been visited by an angel, but Joachim asked them to look at the picture carefully.

"Can you see anything you haven't seen before?" he asked.

They peered at the picture.

Papa said he might not have noticed everything when the bookseller gave them the calendar. He had been so flustered that he had left his driver's license on the counter. For instance, he hadn't noticed that one of the shepherds was holding a shepherd's crook in his hand.

"I don't think I had noticed the little angel either," remarked Mama.

"Of course not!" said Joachim. "Because he hasn't been there till now. And that's because it's a magic Advent calendar."

"Joachim, there's no need to exaggerate," objected Papa.

He always liked to seem the most sensible.

The last thing Joachim thought about before he fell asleep was that one of the angels in heaven was called Joachiel—almost the same as himself.

☽ ☆

THE next morning, Joachim opened the eleventh door in the Advent calendar. He had to coax the thin piece of paper out before he discovered a picture of a horse and rider.

He made himself comfortable under the covers and began to read. Today he did not need to be afraid that Mama or Papa would catch him red-handed, because the secret pieces of paper in the calendar were not so secret anymore.

BALTHAZAR

Five sheep, two shepherds, two angels, one King of the Orient, and a little girl from Norway were speeding up the Valley of the Rhine 1199 years after Jesus was born. They could just glimpse a church tower on the other side of the river. Ephiriel told them it was Mainz Cathedral.

They paused to discuss the situation.

"We have to cross the river," said Joshua. "And that's a pity, because we shall have to frighten another poor ferryman and explain that we're pilgrims on our way to the Holy Land."

"We shall have to try to do it gently," said Ephiriel.

"I can see a boat down there," Impuriel exclaimed.

He flew high in the air, beating his short wings in the direction of the boat, with the rest of the procession after him. But Impuriel was already talking to a man who was sitting on the riverbank. "Can you row us across? We're going all the way to Bethlehem, and we don't have much time if we're to get there before Jesus is born. We're on a godly errand, you see."

Ephiriel hurried after him. When he had caught up with Impuriel, he nodded apologetically at the ferryman. Then he turned to Impuriel and said, "How many times do I have to remind you that first of all you must say, 'Fear not'?"

But the ferryman, who was splendidly dressed in a long red cloak, was not scared by the cherub. He turned to Ephiriel and said, "My name is Balthazar, Second Wise Man and King of Sheba. I'm going the same way as you."

"Then you are one of us," said Ephiriel.

Still, he scolded Impuriel a little. "This time, things turned out well. But you must always start by saying, 'Fear not.' Don't you realize that many people are terribly frightened when they see one of the angels of the Lord, especially when we beat our wings."

"Sorry!" said Impuriel.

"All right, all right," said Ephiriel.

"But isn't it odd that they should be so frightened just because they've seen an angel?" argued Impuriel. "I've never so much as harmed a cat. On the contrary, I couldn't count all the times I've helped a poor cat down from a tall tree. Of course, cats ought to learn once and for all not to climb too high, but when we do come and help them, they're not the tiniest bit frightened. It's always humans who are so terribly nervous."

The two Wise Men embraced.

"It's been a very long time," said the one.

"And it was a very, very long way from the Rhine," said the other.

"But it's very, very, very pleasant to see you again."

They had their arms around each other, so it was not easy to say who had said what. But now the whole procession boarded the boat. The Kings of the Orient each took an oar and rowed across the river, which was almost as wide as a stretch of ocean.

On the other side, Ephiriel pointed at the beautiful cathedral. It seemed a little squatter and did not have as tall a tower as many of the other churches they had passed, but it was much older.

"The year is 1186 after Christ. Work on this cathedral began more than two hundred years ago. At that time, almost a thousand years had passed since the one seed was sown in the earth so that a field of churches and cathedrals would grow across the whole world."

"A whole field of churches!" repeated Impuriel. "It would be fun to work out how much stone and timber have been used to celebrate Jesus' birth. Not to mention how many cakes have been baked or how many presents have been wrapped. Christmas is the world's biggest birthday party, because everybody in the whole world is invited. That's why the party has lasted for thousands of years."

Joshua struck the ground with his crook. "To Bethlehem! To Bethlehem!"

The pilgrims hurried along the west bank of the Rhine. It was very early in the morning, so that very few people would be scared by them.

But when they tumbled into the town of Worms in the year of Our Lord 1162, they met a rider on horseback. Perhaps he was a soldier who had been out on night duty.

The angel Impuriel flew over to the man, beat his wings, and repeated, "Fear not! Fear not! Fear not!"

Even though he buzzed around the soldier like an excited bumblebee and said "Fear not!" an enormous number of times, the poor man was extremely scared. He spurred his horse and galloped around some low buildings. He didn't even have time to say "Hallelujah" or "God be praised."

Ephiriel shook his head in despair and tried to teach the cherub once more. "You only need to say it once. But you must say it in a gentle, soft, heavenly voice. 'Fe-ear no-ot!' you must say. It's a good idea to keep your arms down, too. We do that to show we're not carrying weapons."

Balthazar the Wise Man pointed up at a cathedral with six towers.

"Everywhere and at all times, people have stretched their arms out to God," he said. "The church towers point up to heaven, too, but they last much longer."

The shepherds bent their heads respectfully at these wise words, and Elisabet felt she had to repeat them to herself before she was quite certain what he meant.

Joshua said, "To Bethlehem! To Bethlehem!"

In the city of Basle, on the southern bank of the Rhine, they stopped in front of another big cathedral.

"1119 years have passed since the Christ Child was born," announced Ephiriel. "This cathedral with five naves has just celebrated its centenary. But for hundreds of years Basle has been an important crossroads for travelers who journey through the Alps between Italy and Northern Europe. We are going to follow the same route over the St. Bernard Pass."

"To Bethlehem!" said Joshua the shepherd, striking his crook on the ground. "To Bethlehem!"

Whereupon they set off up through the Swiss mountains.

☽ ☆

JOACHIM sat in bed, thinking about the strange pilgrimage to Bethlehem. After a while Mama and Papa came in to read what was on the piece of paper.

Yesterday they had talked about the magic Advent calendar almost the whole afternoon. Now Papa said, "We took home a small miracle from the bookstore, didn't we, Joachim? Can you imagine how it was made?"

"I think John made it," said Joachim.

"The bookseller said something about someone called John, didn't he?"

Joachim wondered whether he ought to tell Mama and Papa that he had met John. But he didn't. He thought he had to keep one little secret for himself. Because there was something else as well: SABET . . . TEBAS . . . SABET . . . TEBAS.

"If a flower seller has made this calendar," said Papa, "he's certainly inventive."

Mama agreed. "Yes, he is very imaginative."

Joachim sat up in bed. "You said *I* was imaginative when I told you about Elisabet and Ephiriel," he said. "But I'd only read all the scraps of paper that were in the Advent calendar."

"And now we're saying that the person who made the Advent calendar is very imaginative," said Mama. "In a way, it's the same."

Joachim shook his head. "He may not be so imaginative if the story is true."

Papa laughed. "You don't really think you can run all the way to Bethlehem and far back in time as well?"

"Nothing is impossible for God," said Joachim.

Nobody protested. Papa thought they should take out a large atlas so that they could follow Elisabet's journey on the map. He had a historical atlas, a book of maps that showed what all the countries and all the places were called long ago. The same country and the same town have often had many different names, he explained.

Suddenly Mama gasped. "Do you remember that old story from way back?" she said to Papa. "There really was a little girl who disappeared from this town while she and her mother were out doing their Christmas shopping. I think she was called Elisabet."

Papa nodded. "It was some time after the war. Was she called Elisabet?"

"I think so," said Mama, "but I'm not sure."

Suddenly it was as if Mama and Papa had forgotten Joachim. They were so busy talking to each other.

"So maybe he's remembered that old story and made up the rest," suggested Papa. "If it *is* this flower seller who's made it."

Joachim tried to get a word in edgewise. "Can you find out whether she was called Elisabet?"

"Yes, I should think so," said Papa. "Not that it really matters what she was called."

The last person to say anything before they had to hurry to eat breakfast was Joachim. "I think it matters a lot," he said. "Because the lady in the photograph was called Elisabet, too."

12

❦ DECEMBER 12 ❦

. . . for there's no sense in believing
what's right unless it leads to helping
people in distress . . .

WHEN Papa came home from work on December 11, Mama and Joachim jumped on him as soon as he came into the hall and immediately started to talk about the girl who had disappeared.

"Have you found out what her name was?" asked Joachim.

"Let me in first," complained Papa. "Yes, she was called Elisabet. Elisabet Hansen, in fact. It happened in December 1948."

Mama had dinner ready, so they sat down at the table.

"I went into the bookshop as well," continued Papa. "I went into the storeroom with the bookseller . . ."

Mama looked astonished. "Why?"

" . . . and there he found the photo that the flower seller had once put in his window in exchange for a glass of water. I have it in my briefcase."

Papa put the picture on the table. Joachim snatched it and Mama leaned over to look.

It showed a young woman with long fair hair. Around her neck she was wearing a silver cross set with a red stone. She was leaning against a small car. At the top of the photo was a large dome. At the bottom was written "Elisabet."

"Hm, no last name," said Papa. "It's not exactly an unusual name. But it's in Norwegian. In many countries, Elisabet is spelled differently."

Mama looked at him. "So you don't think she's Norwegian?"

"No idea," said Papa. "But look at the photo carefully. The dome in the background is St. Peter's Basilica in Rome. She's standing on the street that leads to St. Peter's Square. The car dates from the end of the fifties."

"I feel almost scared," whispered Mama. "What are we getting mixed up in?"

Papa put his elbows on the table. "Yes, it's a mystery. But there's no reason to believe that the girl who disappeared in 1948 is the woman in the photograph."

He was staring in front of him. "He wasn't at the market," he said.

"Who? You're talking in riddles," said Mama.

"The flower seller . . . John . . . the man with the glass of water. I'd give a lot to talk with him. There's one thing we can take for granted: he made this strange calendar. Now he's disappeared."

Joachim was thinking about everything so much that he wanted to go to bed early. Then it wouldn't be so long before it was morning again and he'd get to know more about Elisabet Hansen and the angel Ephiriel.

When he woke up on December 12, Mama and Papa were in his room before he had opened his eyes. That was unusual because it was Saturday, and Joachim was usually up before the others.

"You are the one who opens the calendar, Joachim," said Papa.

It was obvious that he would have liked to open it himself.

The picture was of a man in a red tunic. He was holding a large sign.

Mama and Papa sat on the bed. Joachim began to read the paper that had fallen out of the calendar.

QUIRINIUS

The five sheep had crossed a ridge and were running down into fertile farmland. Impuriel fluttered around the little flock, and after the sheep and the cherub came Jacob and Joshua, Caspar and Balthazar, Ephiriel and Elisabet.

They passed Lake Biel, and then several more lakes. The biggest and most beautiful was the Lake of Geneva. It glittered so much that it looked as if a piece of heaven had fallen down to earth. Only when Elisabet looked up and saw that there was no hole in the sky was she certain that the picture of the sky in the big lake was only a reflection.

Again they followed an old road alongside a river in a deep valley. Ephiriel told them that the river was called the Rhône and that all the water it carried with it from the Alps ran down first into the Lake of Geneva and later right down to the Mediterranean.

They ran across an old bridge to the other side of the river and stopped in front of a monastery called St. Maurice. There were high Alps on every side, with snow on their peaks.

"The time is 1079 after Christ," said Ephiriel. "The monks have lived here among these tall mountains, praising God and His creation, ever since the seventh century. The monastery is built around the grave of the holy

St. Maurice, who was killed here in this valley in the year 285 because he refused to worship the Roman gods."

He had just finished speaking when a monk walked out of the monastery. He greeted them with a slight nod. "Gloria Dei," he said.

"And the same to you," said Elisabet, even though she had not understood what the monk was saying. She felt that someone ought to answer him.

Only then did the monk notice the two angels. He knelt on the grass and said, "Hallelujah! Hallelujah!"

Clearly, they weren't used to angels visiting the monastery, though it was so high up in the Alps that it was almost the nearest neighbor to the angels in heaven.

Impuriel rose half a meter off the ground, flew toward the monk, gently beating his wings, and said in a voice soft as silk, "Fear not, and be in no wise afraid. We are only going on a short journey to Bethlehem to greet the Christ Child."

Then King Caspar of Nubia strode up to the monk. He said, "Peace be with you and your monastery. As the angel has said, we are on our way to the Holy Land to pay homage to the King of Kings in Bethlehem, the city of David."

With those words, they set off again. They came to a little place called Martigny, where there was an old Roman theater.

"The Romans used this route over the Alps, too," explained the angel Ephiriel. "Much later, Napoleon crossed the Alps with his army."

"To Bethlehem!" called Joshua, and they sped up toward the high mountains. The air was so thin and so clear that Elisabet had to ask herself if she was on the way to heaven. A few times, they saw a mountain hare, a marmot, or an Alpine goat. Up in the sky, crows and vultures circled, and now and again a grouse started up from the bushes.

At the top of the mountain pass stood a large house.

"The year is 1045 after Christ," said the angel Ephiriel. "That house is a hospice. The monks who live here are to look after people who are crossing the Alps. It's brand-new and has been built by Bernard of Menton. At this time—and even in your time, Elisabet—the Benedictine monks live up here and organize rescue missions for people who get lost in the mountains. They are helped by their clever St. Bernard dogs."

"Right!" said the cherub Impuriel. "For Jesus wanted to teach humans to help one another when they were in distress. Once he told a story about a man who was on his way from Jerusalem to Jericho. He was attacked by robbers, who left him half dead at the side of the road. Several priests passed by, but none of them bent down to help the poor man, who was in danger of losing his life. Jesus thought there wasn't much point in their being priests if they couldn't even be bothered to help a fellow human being in distress. They might just as well forget all their pious prayers."

Elisabet nodded, and Impuriel continued, "But then a Samaritan came along, and Samaritans weren't very popular in Judea. It was because they had a religion that was a little different from that of the Jews. But the Samaritan was compassionate and helped the unfortunate man, so that he survived. *Yes indeed!* For there's no sense in believing what's right unless it leads to helping people in distress."

Elisabet nodded again and hid the cherub's words in her heart.

At one point, where the pass forked, a man was standing with a large sign in his hand. He was wearing a long red tunic.

On the sign was written TO BETHLEHEM in capital letters. An arrow had been drawn as well, to show which route they should follow.

"A living road sign!" exclaimed Elisabet.

Ephiriel nodded. "Verily I say unto you, that road sign must be one of us."

Impuriel was so excited that he flew right up to the man and shouted at him, "Fear not! Fear not! Fear not!"

But the man with the sign was not the least bit afraid. He took a step toward Elisabet, offered her his hand, and said, "Congrat . . . no, no, that wasn't quite correct. I mean, at your service, my friends! The very first thing I must remember is to say my name . . . because I, too, have been allowed to take part in this Advent calendar . . . My name is Quirinius, Governor of Syria . . . Attractive appearance, closer acquaintance desired . . . Well, well, the most important thing is, of course, to be good and kind. Dixi!"

Elisabet couldn't help laughing; he talked so oddly. It was as if there were two people talking at once, for he interrupted himself the whole time. He handed her the sign, which he had perhaps been standing and holding for an eternity, with the wind flapping his tunic. He said, "And this . . . if I may have your attention, my friends . . . for here I have the icing on the cake . . . and this prize is for you. Dixi!"

"The sign is for me?" said Elisabet in astonishment.

And Quirinius replied, "Only the one side . . . I mean, you have to turn it . . . around, you understand. Dixi!"

Elisabet didn't understand why he said "Dixi" all the time. It sounded like the name of a dog or cat and there were none in sight. But the angel

Ephiriel whispered that "Dixi" was Latin and meant that Quirinius had finished speaking.

Elisabet turned the sign around and saw to her great surprise that what she was holding in her hand was an Advent calendar with twenty-four doors. Covering all the doors was a picture of a young woman with fair hair. She was standing in front of a church with a large dome on top.

"The first twelve," said Quirinius. "I mean, you may open the first twelve doors . . . for we've come exactly that far . . . on our journey. Dixi!"

She sat down on a rock and opened the first door. Behind it was a picture of a lamb. Behind the next door was an angel, and behind the third a sheep. Then there were pictures of a shepherd, another sheep, a King of the Orient, a sheep, a shepherd, a sheep, a cherub, and another King of the Orient. Elisabet saw that these were pictures of everyone who had joined the pilgrimage on its long way through Europe.

But who was the woman?

"Thank you very much!" she said.

Quirinius shook his head. "On the contrary! You're wrong about that . . . you don't need to say thank you . . . I do. I thank you and the others here . . . for allowing an old Roman like myself . . . to join this godly group . . . which is on the right way to Bethlehem. After all, it was not I . . . in fact, it was you . . . who set off first after the delightful lamb. Dixi! Dixi! Dixi!"

Elisabet looked up at Ephiriel and laughed.

"But you haven't opened the twelfth door," said the angel.

Elisabet opened the twelfth door, and now she was looking down at a tiny picture of the same calendar she was holding. And here, too, there was a picture of a fair-haired woman in front of the dome of a big church.

Joshua struck his shepherd's crook against a cairn. "To Bethlehem! To Bethlehem!"

"How far is it to Bethlehem now?" asked Elisabet.

"Not very far!" said Ephiriel.

☽ ☆

THEY sat looking at each other.

Then Joachim began to laugh. "I hope Quirinius is going all the way to Bethlehem with them," he said.

Mama and Papa examined the thin piece of paper. "He's brought the young woman in front of St. Peter's Square into the story of little Elisabet today," said Papa.

"And then he's made a little Advent calendar inside the big one," said Mama.

"Do you think there's another calendar inside the little Advent calendar?" asked Joachim.

"Who knows?" said Mama. "Who knows?"

*. . . just as lightning sweeps across
the sky, flooding the landscape with light
for a second or two . . .*

WHEN Joachim woke up on December 13, Mama and Papa were in his room already.

"You get to open it, Joachim," said Papa.

Joachim sat up and fished out the folded piece of paper. The picture in the calendar showed a rainbow.

He sat in bed with Mama on one side and Papa on the other. They both leaned over to see. Mama began to read.

THE SIXTH SHEEP

A party of monks who were on their way up from Val d'Aosta one day in June in the year 998 saw a group of pilgrims for a short moment—just as lightning sweeps across the sky, flooding the landscape with light for a second or two.

"Look!" exclaimed one of the monks.

"What?" asked the other.

"I thought I saw a strange procession on its way down through the valley. There were people and animals. Behind them all ran a little girl with an angel."

The third monk agreed. "I saw them, too. It was like a heavenly host."

The monk who had seen nothing shook his head in disbelief. "Are you sure you can stand the thin air up here?" he asked.

He said that because he had looked down at an azalea at the instant when the pilgrimage had passed.

Four years earlier, a party of merchants from Milan had seen the same thing as the two monks. That had been a little farther down the valley.

The godly throng stopped for a little while to enjoy the view of the beautiful Val d'Aosta. Ephiriel pointed up at Mont Blanc, and the sharp peak of the Matterhorn. Elisabet was more interested in studying the Advent calendar she had been given by the Governor of Syria.

She pointed at door number 12, on which there was a picture of an Advent calendar exactly like the one she had in her hand. She turned to Quirinius and asked, "Can I open the doors in the tiny calendar as well?"

Quirinius shook his head. "Unfortunately not. That calendar is sealed with seven seals. Dixi!"

Caspar cleared his throat, and so did Balthazar. "As Wise Men, we can reveal what is inside, all the same," said the first Wise Man. "Something mysterious is written in tiny letters."

"Tell me, then!" said Elisabet.

"Behind the first door is written 'Elisabet,' " Caspar began. "Behind the second is written 'Lisabet,' and behind the third 'Isabet.' Then come Sabet, Abet, Bet, and Et. Those are the first seven doors."

Elisabet smiled a wide smile. "And what then?"

The second Wise Man replied, "After that come Te, Teb, Teba, Tebas, Tebasi, Tebasil, and Tebasile. Then there are only ten doors left."

"What's behind them?"

"Elisabet, Lisabet, Isabet, Sabet, Abet, Bet, and Et."

Elisabet had been counting. "But there are still three doors left," she said.

Caspar nodded solemnly. "Behind door number 22 is written 'Roma.' Behind door number 23 is written 'Amor,' and behind door number 24 'Jesus' is written in very beautiful, artistic lettering. One letter is red, the second is orange, the third is yellow, the fourth blue-green, and the fifth indigo-violet. That makes all the colors of the rainbow. For Jesus was like a rainbow."

"Why?"

"When it has been pouring and the sun breaks through the dark clouds, the rainbow appears in the sky. It's just as if a little bit of Jesus is in the air. For Jesus was like a rainbow between heaven and earth."

Joshua lifted up his shepherd's crook and struck a stone with such force that it echoed all around the mountains. "To Bethlehem!" he said. "To Bethlehem!"

And it was as if the mountains replied, " . . . lehem, lehem, lehem . . ."

It didn't take long for them to reach the Po Valley. That is the fertile land formed by the great Po River, which flows from the Italian Alps in the west to the Adriatic Sea in the east. Ephiriel told them that they would be going the same way as the river.

They traveled through the lush countryside until the Po River met another big river called the Ticino. That was near the trading city of Pavia. Ephiriel told them that the angel watch showed 904 and that Pavia already had a law school that was famous throughout Europe.

Joshua was about to strike the ground with his shepherd's crook. But Jacob the shepherd spoke first. He pointed down at a large raft lying by the riverbank, and said, "We'll borrow that."

So the whole long procession of pilgrims jumped on board the raft.

As they were about to push off from the bank, a man came running toward them with a sheep in his arms. "Accept my sincerest offering!" he said.

So six sheep had to be crammed together on the narrow raft.

When they were out on the river, Quirinius said that Elisabet could open door number 13 in the Advent calendar. Behind it was a picture of a man carrying a sheep.

☽ ☆

WHEN Mama finished reading, they sat on the bed for a long while without saying anything.

"Lehem, lehem, lehem!" said Mama at last, almost as if she were singing it.

"Sabet . . . Tebas," said Joachim.

He surprised himself. There it was again! John had in fact mumbled half of

Elisabet's name. And he'd never thought of it before! Then he had said the same half of her name backward.

But why had he done that?

Papa had to say something, too. "If only I could find this flower seller, maybe we'd know how the Advent calendar was made. Or why, for that matter."

"I'm sure it's so as to spread some of the glory of heaven," said Joachim. "I believe the magic Advent calendar is a small part of the glory of heaven that has strayed down to earth. Up there, it's so full of wonderful things that it's very easy for them to spill over."

Mama and Papa laughed. It was only after they read through all the folded sheets of paper that they understood why Joachim had said so many strange things recently.

"I'm thinking about the three monks in Val d'Aosta," said Mama.

Papa and Joachim looked at her. Then she said, "We're sitting here almost like those monks."

Joachim could no longer keep his secret about meeting John. It was as if this last little secret was exploding inside his head. So it was good to let it out.

"John was at the gate one day when I came home from school," he said. "He got our address from the man in the bookstore."

Papa jumped up. "Why didn't you tell us?"

"I didn't think it was important . . . He only wanted to know who I was."

"Yes, yes. But what did he tell you?" said Papa impatiently. "He must have said something about the magic Advent calendar."

"He said it wasn't Christmas yet. Then he said he'd tell me more about Elisabet another time."

Papa nodded. "I'll drop by the market again today. I intend to *meet* this John . . . even if I have to lasso him."

But when he got home, he just threw up his arms. "Gone!" he said. "As if the earth has swallowed him."

All afternoon, Joachim repeated two names inside himself: Elisabet . . . Tebasile . . . Elisabet.

One name was a reflection of the other. But when Joachim looked in the mirror, he saw himself, though the picture in the mirror was reversed.

Could it be a secret message that the two Elisabets were one and the same person? But Tebasile sounded like a proper name, too.

Could there be someone called Tebasile as well?

That evening, Joachim lay for a long time staring at the ceiling before he could relax. In the end, he had to get up and write something clever in his little notebook. It was something he had seen inside his head.

He wrote:

```
S A B E T
A       E
B       B
E       A
T E B A S
```

*. . . long before the child's forefinger
had time to unfold . . .*

ON December 14, Joachim woke up before Mama and Papa. He sat up in bed. Only ten days left till Christmas Eve.

What was going to happen to Elisabet, the angel Ephiriel, and all the others who were going to Bethlehem?

Before he had a chance to open the Advent calendar, Mama and Papa were in his room. Under his arm, Papa had two large atlases.

Joachim opened door number 14. The folded paper fell on the bed, and in the calendar they saw a picture of a raft with people, animals, and angels on it.

"The raft!" said Mama.

They sat on the edge of the bed. That day Joachim read.

ISAAC

Toward the end of the ninth century, a strange raft was sailing on the Po River in the direction of the Adriatic Sea to the east. The country they were sailing through was called Lombardy. On the raft were a small flock of sheep, bleating crossly because they were not allowed to drink the river water. The smallest sheep was running back and forth, and the little bell hanging around its woolly neck tinkled.

Two Wise Men were making wise observations about the beautiful countryside they were sailing through. One of them was black, the other was white. After a long discussion about the blessings of oranges and dates, they agreed that God could not have created a better world—at least, not in six days.

At the back of the raft stood a man in Roman clothes steering with a long pole. Such clothes had only been out of fashion for a short time. He was talking to a small girl who was holding a piece of cardboard in her hands. On one side was written "TO BETHLEHEM"; on the other was a picture of a young woman with long, fair hair.

Most conspicuous were two angels on the front of the raft, beating their wings to keep the raft from drifting toward the riverbank. This was long before boats were equipped with propellers.

Now and again, the cherub Impuriel turned to the others and praised the beauty of the landscape they were passing.

"Wonderful!" he called out. "Nothing but glory and joy. It's just as on the fifth day, when God saw everything that He had made. And behold—it was good!"

Once or twice, somebody on the shore noticed them. But the raft was seen only for a brief second. That's because it wasn't just sailing down the Po River. It was sailing through history, too. It was crossing the tidal wave of time. When a little child stood on the bank of the river and pointed at the strange raft so that his Mama or Papa would see it, too, it disappeared long before the child's forefinger had time to unfold.

So perhaps it was only a mirage.

They passed old Roman bridges and buildings, theaters, temples, and aqueducts. Ephiriel pointed at all the churches.

"I was often in this area as a young man," Quirinius told them, staring down at the long pole in the water. "But that was a very long time ago . . . or the opposite, of course . . . I mean, it's still a good while before we get there. Dixi!"

Elisabet realized that he was talking about Roman times, when there were Roman soldiers nearly everywhere in the world.

"What did it look like here then?" she asked.

"The Roman theaters are still standing. The orange trees as well—and the red poppies along the riverbank. But nobody had heard about Jesus. What's new are all the churches and monasteries, priests and monks. Dixi! Dixi!"

Before long, Joshua pointed at the riverbank. "We'll land over there."

Quirinius steered the raft toward land, helped by the two angels, who beat their wings energetically. While Joshua the shepherd latched on to a tree with his crook and drew the raft to shore, the angel Ephiriel said a few warning words to the cherub Impuriel.

"If we meet any people, you must be sure to remember to say 'Fear not' in a gentle angel voice, so they will not be afraid. We're only visiting, so it's important that we behave properly."

The pilgrims alighted from the raft. They passed a country church and turned uphill through the countryside.

The towns were not very large at this time, but soon they were approaching one of the largest. Ephiriel told them it was called Padua.

Just before they sped through the town gate, they saw a man in a blue tunic. He was sitting on a stone, with his head in his hands. It looked as if he had been sitting there for a very long time.

Impuriel flew toward him, hovered in the air right in front of him, fluttering his wings, and said, "Fear not and be in no wise afraid. I, Impuriel, am one of God's angels who is out on a godly errand."

It looked as if the cherub's words had an effect, for the man did not throw himself to the ground and hide his head. He said neither "Hallelujah" nor "Gloria Dei." He simply got to his feet and walked toward them.

"Then he is one of us," said Ephiriel.

The man offered his hand to Elisabet. "I am Isaac the shepherd and I am going the same way as you."

That made it much easier to guide the six sheep through Padua. They were followed by three shepherds, two Kings of the Orient, two angels, one governor, and a little girl from Norway. Altogether, there were fifteen of them.

They were going so fast that the few people who were out in the streets didn't have time to look at them before they vanished. The pilgrims only just managed to see the inhabitants of the town, too. When they glimpsed an early riser, the man or woman disappeared in the next instant—and was perhaps replaced by a different man or woman.

Elisabet thought they were in the town for only half a minute, but in fact the strange pilgrimage haunted the streets of Padua for seven or eight long years; for that half minute consisted of thirty brief seconds, and those thirty brief seconds were divided among all those seven or eight years.

Ancient accounts tell us that there was never so much talk of angels in Padua as during those magic years from 804 to 811. Now and then, someone or other thought they had seen something strange in the streets. Could it have been a procession of angels who had swept through the town?

Outside the town walls, they stopped in front of a small monastery.

"Strange to see a Roman town again," said Quirinius. "I wonder who's the emperor now."

Ephiriel looked at his angel watch. "It's exactly 800 years after Christ. On Christmas Day this year, Charles the Great will be crowned Emperor of the West."

"Then we'll soon be starting on a new century," said Joshua the shepherd. He struck his shepherd's crook against the monastery wall. "To Bethlehem! To Bethlehem!"

☽ ☆

PAPA opened the atlas, pointed out the Po River, and found the town of Padua. Then he turned the pages backward and forward and with his finger tried to trace the long distance the pilgrims had run.

"Here's Halden," he began. "Then they came down to the big lake in Sweden . . . That must be Vänern. From there, they hurried south through Sweden to Kungälv, Göteborg, Halmstad, and Lund. They rowed across to Sjaelland and visited Copenhagen. Yes, I can find it all. They arrived in Fyn and leaped through Odense. From Middelfart they were ferried across the Little Belt to Jutland. There they passed the towns of Kolding and Flensburg . . ."

"They traveled back in history as well," said Mama.

But Papa went on following the path they had run, with his finger on the map.

"Here's Hamburg. Then Elisabet was left lying in the market in Hanover . . . yes, here. And here's Hamelin, the town that had broken its solemn promise to the rat catcher."

"You broke a solemn promise, too," interrupted Joachim. "You opened my secret box."

Papa continued, "Farther south is Paderborn; this is where the cherub Impuriel flew down in spirals from the church tower. From there, they ran to Cologne and continued up the Rhine Valley. And Impuriel was quite right: it's wondrously beautiful there."

"That was during the thirteenth century," said Mama.

"Wait a moment," said Papa. "I want to follow the whole route. In Mainz, they met Balthazar . . . Then it was Worms and Basle. Today Basle is in Switzerland . . ."

"But Elisabet was there around 1100," said Mama again.

Papa went on searching with his finger. "Here's Lake Biel . . . and the Lake of Geneva. I've found the little place called Martigny . . . This is a good map. Through the St. Bernard Pass, yes . . . today there are tunnels all over the place. Down through Val d'Aosta . . . to Lombardy and the Po Valley."

"Bravo!" said Mama. "But they're traveling through history as well. I think *that* journey is an even stranger one to think about."

Only now did Papa look up from his map. "But the flower seller made that up."

"I think it's true," said Joachim.

Mama nodded. "Yes, who knows?"

Papa only shook his head. "Now I wonder which route they're going to take . . ."

"It's eight o'clock!" exclaimed Mama.

There was some quarreling and scolding because they were so short of time. That's what Joachim called stress, and he thought nothing was worse.

As he ran to school, many strange names were buzzing in his head. He had now seen all those places on the map.

At school, they had started to rehearse the Nativity play; Joachim's class would be putting it on in the gym on the last schoolday before Christmas. Joachim was going to be the Second Shepherd.

15

❧ DECEMBER 15 ❧

. . . "Fear not,"
he said, in a voice as
soft as silk . . .

WHEN Joachim woke up on December 15, there were only ten doors left to open in the magic Advent calendar. He didn't even have time to sit up in bed before Mama and Papa were in his room.

Joachim was no longer angry because they had opened his secret box. They had done something they had no right to, but he had forgiven them. It would have been boring to sulk about it forever. Besides, it was more fun to read about Elisabet and the pilgrimage with Mama and Papa. It was almost like having a birthday every day until Christmas Eve.

"Let's get going," said Papa.

Neither he nor Mama hid the fact that the magic Advent calendar was just as exciting for them as it was for Joachim.

Joachim sat up and opened door number 15. He carefully fished out the folded pieces of paper. The picture showed islands and reefs, with houses on them; the small islands were bathed in radiant sunshine.

That day, it was Papa's turn to read. He grabbed the thin piece of paper and cleared his throat twice before beginning.

THE SEVENTH SHEEP

Six sheep, three shepherds, three Wise Men, two angels, one Roman governor, and a little girl from Norway came to the Lagoon of Venice at the head of the Adriatic Sea.

They paused on a little rise with a view over the lagoon, and Ephiriel began to point out all the small islands and reefs that studded the water. On many of the islands the Venetians had built houses, on some of them churches as well. Several of the islets were so close together that bridges had been built between them. There were small fishing boats everywhere.

"The year is 797 after Christ," announced Ephiriel. "We see the young Venice, which is what the 118 islands will soon be called. The Venetians settled here for protection from the sea pirates and barbarians who roamed the area. Exactly a hundred years ago, they all combined under a leader who was called the Doge."

"I can't see any gondolas," complained Elisabet. "I thought there would be many more bridges, too."

Ephiriel laughed. "But you're not in the Venice of the twentieth century. I said the time was 797, and people had lived here for only a couple of centuries. But Venice will soon become so thickly populated that one island will scarcely be separate from another."

While they stood looking out over all the islets and islands, a small rowboat glided by. One end of the rowboat was filled with salt. At the other end stood some sheep, bleating at the sun, which was about to break through the morning mist.

The man who was rowing the boat was so frightened when he saw the procession of pilgrims that he covered his eyes with his arm, took a step back, lost his balance, and fell head over heels into the water. Elisabet saw him come to the surface a few seconds later and then go under again.

"He's drowning!" she called. "We must save him."

The angel Ephiriel was already on his way. He hovered gracefully above the glittering water, seized the man when he surfaced again, and lifted him up on land. The water poured off him. Ephiriel pulled in the rowboat.

The man whose fear had nearly caused him to drown lay down on the ground and coughed fit to burst. He gasped for breath and said, "*Gratie, gratie . . .*"

Elisabet tried to explain that they were on their way to Bethlehem to greet the Christ Child and that he needn't be afraid. Impuriel had begun circling around him.

"Fear not," he said, in a voice as soft as silk, "and be in no wise afraid. But you should not have been all alone on the sea if you can't swim, for you can't expect an angel to be around all the time. We only very rarely wander about, you know."

It didn't look as if Impuriel's advice was any comfort to the man. But the cherub sat down beside him, patted him on the cheek, and went on repeating "Fear not." It seemed to be having an effect, for the man got to his feet and trudged back to his boat. He lifted a little lamb out of it and walked back toward them.

"Agnus Dei," he said.

That means "God's lamb," and the lamb joined the rest of the flock without protest. Joshua struck his shepherd's crook on the ground and said, "To Bethlehem! To Bethlehem!"

They went off again. At the very end of the Gulf of Venice stood the old Roman town of Aquileia.

As they ran, Ephiriel pointed to a monastery. "The year is 718 after Christ. But there have been Christian communities here from ancient times."

The procession of pilgrims sped on through the town of Trieste. Then they continued south, across country, through Croatia.

☽ ☆

PAPA put the scrap of paper down on the bed and opened one of the large atlases that he had placed on Joachim's desk.

"Here's Venice," he said, "and here's Trieste; that's on the border of Yugoslavia. I can't find Aquileia."

"But maybe it doesn't exist anymore," said Mama. "You have to look in the historical atlas."

Papa went to get the other large atlas. There were many maps of all the countries in Europe, but the names of the countries and the towns were different from one map to the other.

"Look for a map of the area in the eighth century," said Mama.

Papa turned the pages of the atlas. "Here it is! Aquileia! The old town was situated halfway between Venice and Trieste. This is fantastic . . ."

"What is?" asked Joachim.

"John must have used old maps like this, too. For the world changes all the time. History is like a big pile of pancakes and each pancake is a different map of the world."

"Pancakes?" said Joachim.

Papa nodded. "It's never enough to ask where something's happening. It's not enough to ask when something's happening, either. You have to ask both when and where."

He put his hands on Joachim's hands. "Imagine that you have twenty pancakes piled on top of each other. If there's a black speck on one of the pancakes, and you have to find that particular speck, you must find out which of the twenty pancakes the black speck is on and exactly where on the pancake. You may have to search through the whole pile."

Joachim nodded, and Papa went on, "The long journey to Bethlehem goes right through all twenty pancakes. Because Elisabet doesn't just travel around on the top pancake. She's moving through the entire pancake mountain."

Now Joachim understood what Papa meant.

"They're traveling down through twenty centuries," said Papa finally. "There are maps in this book that show exactly how the world looked in every one of the twenty centuries. I think John must have been reading a pancake book like this."

When he said "pancake book," he and Joachim couldn't help laughing.

"The big question is whether there really *was* a man who was saved by an angel in Venice in the year 797. Do you think we could find out?" said Mama.

"You don't really think this story is *true*?" said Papa.

"No, I guess not," said Mama, wavering. "But if it really *had* happened, the man would have talked about it, to a priest, for instance. Then it would have been written down somewhere. Maybe we should search through the library."

Papa wouldn't hear such talk. He said, "Let's go and have a pizza in town and visit the market afterwards. Do you remember what he looks like, Joachim?"

"Of course," said Joachim. "I'd recognize him at once. He talked with an accent, but then, he probably isn't Norwegian."

☽ ☆

THAT day, Mama picked Joachim up at school. They took the bus to town and met Papa. From the pizza restaurant they could look down on the market in front of the cathedral.

As they ate, Papa kept asking, "Do you see him, Joachim?"

Every time, Joachim had to answer no, because John wasn't at the market selling flowers.

They bought some special candles and a couple of Christmas presents. Then they went into the bookstore where Joachim had found the magic Advent calendar.

The old man recognized Papa and Joachim at once, and shook Mama's hand, too.

"Here we are again," said Papa. "We wondered whether you had seen anything of this remarkable flower seller."

The bookseller shook his head. "He hasn't been here for quite a while. At this time of year he's often not around as much."

"The magic Advent calendar is a bit of a mystery," explained Mama. "We wanted to invite him to our house, to thank him properly for it."

They agreed that the bookseller should ask John to phone them.

As they were about to leave, Papa said, "Just one more thing. Do you know what country he comes from?"

"I think he said he was born in Damascus," said the bookseller.

In the car going home, Papa drummed his fingers on the steering wheel. "If only we had found that man!" he said.

"At least we found out where he comes from," said Mama. "Isn't Damascus the capital of Syria?"

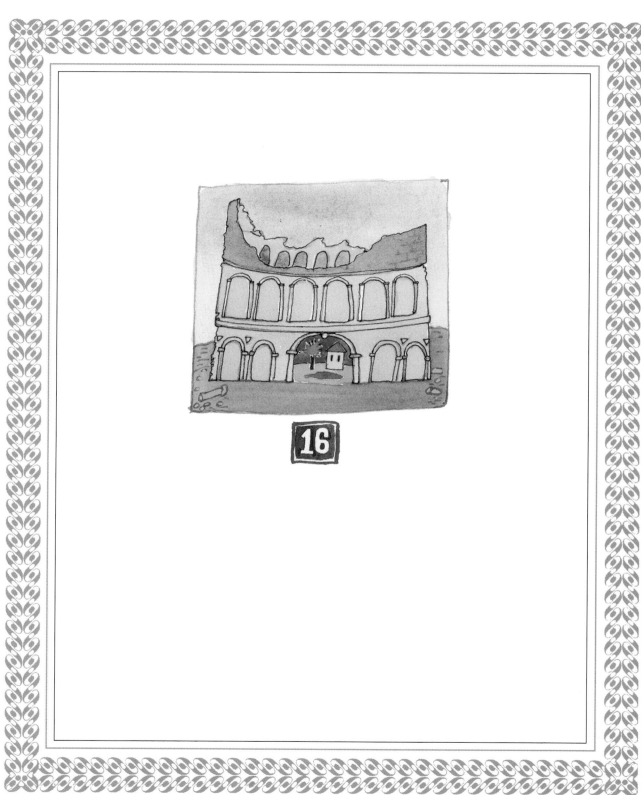

16

❧ DECEMBER 16 ❧

*. . . it was as if
he was suffering from
a holy hiccup . . .*

FOR the rest of the evening, they talked about Elisabet, John, and the magic Advent calendar. Even when nobody said anything, they all knew what the others were thinking about.

Papa would drop a fork on the floor as he was clearing the dinner table, and say, "Too bad we can't find him. But I expect he's an old fox, and old foxes are very difficult to catch."

Mama would be sitting with the newspaper on her lap, staring straight ahead, and say, "After all, it's a mystery in itself why that little girl never came back."

Joachim had put the photo of the grownup Elisabet on the mantelpiece. In the middle of the children's program, he would look up from the television at the old photograph and say, "Maybe she was his girlfriend."

Mama and Papa heard what he said. Papa put his cup on the coffee table. "Yes, maybe."

"Because inside that tiny Advent calendar," said Mama, "the one inside the Advent calendar that Quirinius gave Elisabet, was written, not just Elisabet and Tebasile. There was Roma and Amor as well. Amor means love."

Joachim turned off the TV and jumped up from his chair. "It really means something?"

Mama nodded. "Yes. Amor means love."

"But that's Roma backward," Joachim said. "So perhaps Tebasile really means something as well."

☽ ☆

EARLY on the morning of December 16, Mama and Papa appeared in Joachim's room.

"Wake up, Joachim," said Mama. "It's only seven o'clock, but we need some extra time together these days."

Joachim rubbed the sleep out of his eyes and looked up at all the doors in the Advent calendar.

He thought again that having the magic Advent calendar was like having a birthday every day. Would it be possible to make a calendar like that to last the whole year, he wondered.

He remembered something he had dreamed. A little girl had crawled down through a giant batch of pancakes to look for something she had lost. In the end, she found it on the pancake at the very bottom. It was a tiny doll wrapped in cloth. In the dream the doll was alive.

Joachim found the door with the number 16 on it. The folded piece of paper fell out on the bed, and Papa picked it up. Behind the door was a picture of an old castle.

"I'll read it," said Mama. It was her turn.

DANIEL

It happened in the days when the old Roman Empire was divided in two. In both East and West, the Christian religion had taken root. But the Christian world was still being plundered by heathen peoples. They delayed the building of new churches, stole gold and silver, and pillaged whole cities.

A decree was sent out from the Pope in Rome that the Church's property should be defended against the foreigners who had not yet heard about Jesus. That was when a strange procession advanced through time and space on its way to Bethlehem, the city of David. They came from a distant future.

At Salonae in Dalmatia they stopped in front of the ancient ruins of a Roman imperial palace. At first the ruins seemed abandoned, but the godly company entered by way of a small gate in the wall and discovered that the place was teeming with people. It was like tearing the bark off an old log to see small insects creeping around inside. In the middle of the old imperial palace, a small town had been built.

When the angel Ephiriel saw all the people in the town he said, "The angel watch says 688 after Christ. We are standing inside the walls of the palace of the Emperor Diocletian. Diocletian was born in this part of the country about 250 years after Christ. He fought against the nomadic tribes and tried to rebuild the old Roman Empire. He closed the Christian churches and persecuted the Christians cruelly. When he died in 316, he was buried here in the great palace. But by the end of the century the whole of the Roman Empire became Christian. A town grew up inside the old palace of the Emperor. Much later, this town will be called Split."

While the angel Ephiriel was talking, a little boy noticed them. He was wearing almost no clothes. He pointed at them and called out, "*Angelos! Angelos!*"

"What does that mean?" Elisabet asked Ephiriel.

"It means angels. I don't suppose he's met very many of us before."

The next moment, all the people had seen them. The children stood still and gazed up in amazement, but the grownups threw themselves down, murmuring "Gloria," "Amen," and "Hallelujah" over and over again.

Impuriel hovered above their heads. "Be not in the slightest bit afraid," he said. "For 688 years ago there was born unto you in Bethlehem, the city of David, the best saviour ever. Now we are traveling from the four corners of the earth to pay Him homage."

A man in black clothes came toward them. "The priest," whispered Ephiriel.

He said something that Elisabet didn't understand, but the angel explained that he was asking them to greet the Christ Child from this corner of the world, too.

Joshua struck his shepherd's crook against the old town wall and said, "To Bethlehem! To Bethlehem!"

They hurried on down through Dalmatia. They leaped over hills and ridges and had many good views of the Adriatic Sea.

Ephiriel pointed to a harbor town below. "The time is 659. That little town is called Ragusa and has just been founded by Greeks from the Peloponnesus. Later, the town will become an important trading and shipping center and will be called Dubrovnik."

On a rise with a view over the sea, they met another shepherd, who was sitting under a pine tree to protect himself from the strong sun. He had the same light blue tunic as Joshua, Jacob, and Isaac. When he saw the procession of pilgrims approaching, he got to his feet and came to meet them.

"Glory to God in the highest," he said. "My name is Daniel and I have been waiting here for many years, but I knew you would pass through Dalmatia sometime during the seventh century. I am coming with you to Bethlehem."

"Yes, indeed!" said Impuriel. "For you are one of us."

Joshua struck his crook against the pine tree. "To Bethlehem! To Bethlehem!"

Soon they came to a large lake. At the end of the lake was a town.

"This town is called Scodra, and the lake is the Lake of Scodra," said Ephiriel. "After many centuries, this land will be called Albania. We have left the Roman Catholic region now and have reached the territory that will be governed from Byzantium."

Elisabet felt confused by all the strange names, but the angel explained, "The angel watch shows that 602 years have passed since Jesus was born. At this time, and throughout the Middle Ages, the Christian Church had two different capitals. The one is Rome, and the other is Byzantium, at the mouth of the Black Sea."

"But didn't they believe the same things?"

"On the whole, yes. But they showed it in slightly different ways. For people have come and gone, and so have church traditions and services. Though the start of it all was something that happened one Christmas night in Bethlehem, the city of David."

Impuriel ruffled his wings and said, "Yes, indeed! For there was only one Mary and only one Christ Child. Since then, many millions of images of Mary and the Christ Child have been painted and chiseled, and no two of them are alike. There was only one Christ Child, but every person's imagination is a little different."

Elisabet hid these words in her heart.

Impuriel beat his wings and came right up to her. "God created only one Adam and one Eve as well. They were little children who played hide-and-seek and climbed the trees in the Garden of Eden. For there was no point in creating a Paradise if there were no children who could play in it. But then these two little rascals ate the fruit of the Tree of Knowledge, and they grew up. That was the end of playing in the world, but only for a short while. Soon grownup Adam and grownup Eve had children of their own, and then grandchildren. In this way, God made sure that there would always be plenty of children in the world. There's no point in creating a whole world if there are no little children to keep on discovering it. That's how God goes on creating the world over and over again. He will never quite finish, for new children keep on arriving, and they discover the world for the very first time. *Yes indeed!*"

The two Wise Men looked at one another.

"Well, well!" said Balthazar.

And Caspar added, "This explanation is perhaps a little dubious. But all good stories may be understood in at least two or three ways, and only one story can be told at a time."

"But even though many billions of children have lived on earth, no two of them have been exactly alike," said Impuriel. "There are no two blades of grass in the whole of creation that are absolutely exactly alike. That's because God in heaven is so full of imagination that every now and again it bubbles over and a little spills onto the earth. 'Fill the waters in the seas, and let birds multiply on the earth,' He said as He slaved away at creating the world in six days. 'Let the earth bring forth the living creature according to its kind: cattle and creeping thing and beast of the earth, *each* according to its kind . . .' "

Impuriel glanced at Elisabet. "I know it all by heart."

Elisabet clapped her hands. She had always found it difficult to learn old stories and rhymes by heart.

Joshua thumped his shepherd's crook on the ground. "To Bethlehem! To Bethlehem!"

On they went, up through the Macedonian highlands.

☽ ☆

WHEN Mama finished reading, they sat smiling at one another.

"This flower seller certainly doesn't lack imagination," said Papa.

He turned the pages of one of the atlases. "They've run through all of Yugoslavia. That's quite a lot for one day."

"For a hundred years, you mean," said Joachim. "Every single day is a hundred years."

"But that's only for us," argued Mama. "For Elisabet and all the others, it goes very fast. Besides, it's not called Yugoslavia anymore. It wasn't in the seventh century either. Then it was called Croatia and Dalmatia."

Papa went on studying the map. He showed Joachim where they had been running. Finally he pointed out the towns of Split and Dubrovnik.

☽ ☆

WHEN Papa came home from work that afternoon, he said, "I went to the police station today."

Mama looked surprised. "To find John?"

Papa shook his head. "No, no. I wanted to find out a little more about this girl who disappeared in 1948. She was only seven years old and she really did vanish. The police searched for her for months, but she never turned up. The only thing they found was her knitted cap. It was lying in the woods just outside the town. So that little girl must have had a brief life."

"I don't think you should be so certain of that," said Mama.

Papa went on, "I contacted her family, too. I made a few phone calls, and finally managed to talk to her mother. She's now an old lady in her seventies."

Mama and Joachim both spoke at once.

"What did she say?"

"Did she know John?"

"One question at a time, please," said Papa. "She couldn't tell me much more than the police. But she did say that once, many, many years ago, she had talked to a man who came from Syria. His name was John. The girl's father died a few years ago. He had traveled to Syria and many other countries. But . . ." Papa took a deep breath. "She *hadn't* heard about the picture that was taken in Rome ten to fifteen years after Elisabet disappeared. I promised to send her a copy."

A few minutes after Mama and Papa said good night, Joachim got out of bed and sat at his desk.

Who was the young woman John had taken a picture of in Rome? Was she called Elisabet—or something else?

"Sabet . . . Tebas . . ." he said. But why did he say that? They sounded almost like sorcerers' words.

Joachim opened his little notebook and looked at the way he had written the two names before. Now he wrote:

```
S A B E T E B A S
A       E       A
B       B       B
E       A       E
T E B A S A B E T
E       A       E
B       B       B
A       E       A
S A B E T E B A S
```

Was that a window? Or was it a cross?

Maybe it was an Advent calendar.

❧ DECEMBER 17 ❧

*. . . many things have
been done in the name of Jesus that
do not please heaven . . .*

ON December 17, Joachim woke up first. He even opened the magic Advent calendar before Mama and Papa got up. The picture was of the entire procession of pilgrims on their way down a steep mountainside.

The minute he had unfolded the thin piece of paper, Papa came in. "You haven't opened it already, have you?" he asked.

Joachim started. "Yes. But I haven't read the piece of paper."

And Papa hurried into the bedroom and got Mama out of bed. She wasn't even allowed to brush her teeth first. They sat down on the edge of the bed and peered at the piece of paper. It was Papa's turn to read.

SERAPHIEL

It was the very end of the sixth century. Across the Macedonian chain of mountains sped a long procession of pilgrims.

Down on the bank of the Axios River, a sheep farmer looked up at the mountains. First he saw the seven godly sheep rolling down the mountainside like a pearl necklace. Around them fluttered a white bird. Behind the sheep came four men, one of them holding a shepherd's crook in his hand. Behind the four shepherds came even more people.

The amazing sight lasted only a second or two. Then it was gone. The sheep farmer rubbed his eyes, but remembered that his father had told him of having a similar vision many years ago, a little farther down the Axios Valley. He had seen a mysterious company escorted by two angels.

Long after the vision of the pilgrims' procession had gone, the sheep farmer realized that the white bird had not been a bird at all. He, too, had seen one of the angels of the Lord.

The pilgrims followed the river down to where it ran out into the Thermaic Gulf in the Aegean Sea. Elisabet had never seen such blue water.

Ephiriel pointed up at a mountain peak far away to the right of the Gulf they were gazing at. "That's Mount Olympus. In the old days, the Greeks believed the gods lived there. They were called Zeus and Apollo, Athena and Aphrodite. But now angel time tells us that 569 years have passed since the birth of Jesus, and no one believes in the Greek gods anymore."

"Do they believe in Jesus?" asked Elisabet.

The angel nodded.

"But it's only about forty years since the Church closed the Academy, the ancient school of philosophy in Athens. That was founded almost a thousand years ago by a famous philosopher called Plato."

"Why did they close the old school?"

Ephiriel said something that Elisabet hid in her heart.

"Many things have been done in the name of Jesus that do not please heaven. Jesus wanted to talk to everyone. He never expected people to keep their opinions to themselves. Only a few years later, Paul came to Athens. He was the first great missionary for Christendom, and when he arrived in Athens he wanted to speak with the Greek philosophers. He asked them to listen to the words of the Lord, but he wanted to hear what they thought as well."

He couldn't say any more because Joshua struck the ground with his shepherd's crook and said, "To Bethlehem! To Bethlehem!"

After a while, they came to a city located at the innermost point of the Gulf. Ephiriel said that the time was 551, that the city was called Thessalonica, and that the Romans had made it the capital of Macedonia.

"As early as fifty years after the birth of Jesus, Paul established a Christian community here. And we're still a long way from the Holy Land. Paul wrote two letters to the Christians in this city. We can read them to this day, for both those letters are in the Bible."

Elisabet thought about the angel's words. She had not realized that it was possible to keep a few letters for so long.

147

They entered the city by the town gate. It was early in the morning and hardly a soul was to be seen in the streets. Ephiriel pointed to the many churches and said that some of them were several hundred years old. He stopped by one of them and said, "Fifteen hundred years shall pass, and this Church of St. George will still stand here."

They sped east and soon came to another city.

"This is Philippi," said Ephiriel. "Here Paul made his first speech on European soil. Here he established the first Christian community in Europe. In the Bible there is a letter which he wrote to the Philippians when he was imprisoned because of his faith."

Ephiriel pointed to an octagonal church. All of a sudden, one of the doors was opened from the inside. Impuriel had already started to say, "Fear not," when out of the octagonal church strode another angel. He took a few steps toward Elisabet and said, "Greetings, my daughter. I am Seraphiel, and I am coming with you to Bethlehem to welcome the Christ Child into the world."

Joshua struck his shepherd's crook against the church wall. "To Bethlehem! To Bethlehem!"

They set off along the old road between the Ionian Sea and Constantinople. Seraphiel told them that the road was called the Via Egnatia.

They stormed eastward. As they ran, Ephiriel said, "The time is 511 after Christ, and we shall be in Constantinople before it's 500."

☽ ☆

PAPA looked in the atlas to see which way the pilgrims had gone. "Here's the Macedonian mountain chain. Then they came down to the Axios River, that's here. And this is the Thermaic Gulf. When they're standing here, they can see Mount Olympus on their right. That's correct. Yes, it all fits."

He opened the second atlas, the one that showed how the countries of Europe had looked in the sixth century. "The Via Egnatia must be this road," he said. "Here you see Thessalonica and Philippi."

"Isn't there a map of Paul's travels?" Mama wanted to know.

Papa paged through the atlas. Joachim thought that was a little magical, too, since it showed how the world had looked in every age. It even showed cities that had been buried in earth and sand many, many years ago.

"Here it is!" exclaimed Papa. He had found the map that showed Paul's four great missionary journeys. "Paul visited Philippi and Thessalonica on his second journey."

☽ ☆

WHEN Joachim came home from school, the telephone was ringing. He thought it must be Mama or Papa because they sometimes called to tell him they would be home a little later, or to say he could find something to eat in the refrigerator. He hated that more than anything.

He lifted the receiver. "Hello?"

"It's John."

What should he say? Joachim thought hard, then repeated the phrase Mama usually used when he had been playing with a friend and had come home much too late.

"Where *have* you been?" he asked.

"I'm somewhere out in the wilderness," John said. "But we can meet some other time. I just wanted to know how it's going with the magic Advent calendar."

"Fine," said Joachim. "It's like having a birthday every day, because now Mama and Papa are reading all the pieces of paper, too. We do it together."

"Is that so? It's still possible to read them, then?"

Joachim didn't understand what he meant.

"We read them every day."

"Fine—yes, that's fine. Where are the pilgrims now?"

"I think it's called Philippi," said Joachim. "We've looked it up on the map."

"That's good. That was the point of it, too."

"Oh?"

"But, Joachim?"

"Yes?"

"What do you think the Greek sheep farmer thought when he saw the angel procession coming down to the Axios Valley?"

"I'm sure he was very frightened," said Joachim.

"You can say that again."

"There are a lot of things Mama and Papa want to ask you about," continued Joachim. "Can you come and have coffee with us?"

John laughed. Then he said, "It's not Christmas yet."

"You can have coffee and cakes anyway. We've baked a lot already."

He was suddenly afraid that John might stop talking, so he quickly asked, "Are you sure the woman in the photo is called Elisabet?"

"I'm almost sure . . ." said John. "If not, she's called Tebasile."

Joachim thought of the strange Advent calendar Quirinius had given Elisabet, and he thought of what John had said when they met by the garden gate.

"Perhaps she's called both," he said. "Perhaps she's called Elisabet Tebasile."

There was a long silence.

"Yes, maybe so. Maybe *so*, yes!"

"Was she Norwegian?"

John sighed. "Yes and no, yes and no. She was from Palestine, from a little village near Bethlehem. She said she was a Palestinian refugee. But it seems she was born in Norway. The whole thing's so strange."

"So she ran to Bethlehem with Ephiriel and the little lamb?" asked Joachim, breathlessly.

"What a lot of questions!" said John. "But now I must hang up. We must learn to wait, you see, Joachim. Did you know that 'Advent' means something that is to come?"

And he hung up!

Joachim couldn't concentrate on anything until Mama and Papa came home. He had to tell them about John's phone call over and over again, because Papa wanted to be absolutely sure John hadn't said anything important that Joachim had forgotten.

"Elisabet Tebasile!" he muttered. "There can't be anyone called that."

But there was something else. Joachim knew that a refugee was someone who had to flee from his or her own country because of war and danger. But he didn't know that anyone had had to flee from Bethlehem.

Papa consulted the atlas again. He told Joachim that many people in the villages around Bethlehem had had to move because of war. Some of them had lost all their possessions and were in such difficulties that they had to live in refugee camps.

"A Good Samaritan should have come to help them," Joachim said. "Because Jesus wanted to teach people to help one another when in need. And then there would have been peace. For peace is the message of Christmas."

❧ DECEMBER 18 ❧

*. . . God's kingdom is open to everyone,
even people who travel without a ticket . . .*

PAPA hadn't liked it that Joachim opened the magic Advent calendar door before he and Mama got up. On December 18 he woke Joachim.

That day, there was a picture of a rod with a shining gold ball on one end.

"That's a scepter," explained Mama. "Kings and emperors use rods like that as a symbol of dignity. The round ball is probably meant to be the sun."

Joachim unfolded the thin piece of paper which had fallen out of the calendar and began to read to Mama and Papa. They sat on either side of him on his bed.

THE EMPEROR AUGUSTUS

Astrange procession swept through Thrace toward Constantinople on the Golden Horn between the Sea of Marmara and the Black Sea. They were going to Bethlehem. Five hundred years had passed since Jesus was born in a stable, was swaddled in cloth and placed in a manger because there was no room for Mary and Joseph in the inn. But that story was familiar all over the world.

They stopped in front of one of the city gates, which were guarded by soldiers. The soldiers drew their swords and raised their spears when the first sheep reached the gate. Then the angel Seraphiel flew up beside the sheep and placed himself between them and the soldiers.

"Be not afraid," he said. "We are on our way to Bethlehem to pay homage to the Christ Child. You must allow us to pass."

The soldiers dropped their weapons and threw themselves on the ground. One of them signaled that the procession could pass through the city gate. Soon the pilgrims were inside the solid city walls.

It was early in the morning, and the city was not yet awake. The procession of pilgrims stopped on a hill with a good view of the harbor and the Bosporus, which divides Europe from Asia. The straits were so narrow that they could see across to the other side.

"The time is 495," said Ephiriel. "Originally, the city was called Byzantium. But in the Year of Our Lord 330 it was made the capital of the Roman Empire by the Emperor Constantine. The city was built to be the new Rome, and it was soon given the name Constantinople. In just under a thousand years, in 1453, the city will be conquered by the Turks, and they will give it the name Istanbul."

"Had the soldiers heard about Jesus?" Elisabet wanted to know.

"We can take that for granted. The Emperor Constantine made Christianity a lawful religion in the Roman Empire as early as 313. He was baptized himself just before he died. Some years later, in 380, Christianity became the state religion throughout the Roman Empire."

"How do you remember all the dates?" asked Elisabet.

"I just have to follow the angel watch," replied Ephiriel. "Since we don't have to bother about seconds, minutes, hours, and days, it's not so difficult to remember the years. Another date we must make note of is the year 395, exactly a hundred years ago. That was when the Roman Empire was divided, and Constantinople became the capital of the Eastern Roman Empire."

The angel Seraphiel came up. He pointed at a beautiful church. "That church is called a basilica," he said, "and was built in honor of God's wisdom by the Emperor Constantine. In a few years, it will be destroyed by fire, but on the same spot the lovely Hagia Sophia will be built. It will stand as a landmark for centuries."

Quirinius cleared his throat. "We must get across the Bosporus," he said. "Then it's not very far to Syria. Dixi!"

Joshua thumped his shepherd's crook on the ground. "To Bethlehem! To Bethlehem!"

They ran down through the city and before long were standing on the farthest point of the Golden Horn. At the edge of the pier they were met by a dignified man in colorful clothes, with a glittering scepter in his hand. In the other hand he was holding a thick book.

Impuriel was already preparing to say "Fear not," but the regal-looking man paid no attention to the cherub. He came straight toward them.

"I am the Emperor Augustus and I will accompany you across the Bosporus. I order you to accept this gesture on my part without any unpleasant protests."

He pointed out a ship with several large sails. The sheep were already jumping on board.

"Then you are one of us," said Ephiriel.

Elisabet turned to the angel and said, "I didn't know the Emperor Augustus was a Christian."

A mysterious smile passed over the angel's face. "The old Roman Emperor has been part of the Christmas gospel as a kind of stowaway for many centuries. And God's kingdom is open to everyone, even people who travel without a ticket."

Elisabet thought the angel's words made heaven seem even bigger than she had imagined. She hid what he had said in her heart.

Soon the pilgrims had crossed the Bosporus. As they landed, Elisabet spoke to the Roman Emperor and asked what kind of book he had under his arm. She thought he was going to say it was the Bible—or at least a hymn book. But the Emperor Augustus said, "It is the sacred census."

He said no more. He was so handsome and so proud and he clearly did not like talking too long at a time, at least not to little girls. Elisabet thought that was odd; surely it wasn't every day that a Roman Emperor was able to meet a girl who had run off after a lamb who had escaped from a big store in Norway and headed for Bethlehem.

Joshua struck the ground with his crook and reminded them that they had to leave. But they hadn't gone very far before they stopped on a hill above the town of Chalcedon.

The town was teeming with priests; they were like a swarm of bees. Elisabet was astonished—in fact, almost scared—to see so many priests at once.

"Fear not," said the angel Seraphiel. "The time is 451 years after the birth of Jesus, and the biggest conference in the history of the Christian Church is being held down there. The town is called Chalcedon, and priests and bishops from the whole of the Christian world are here."

"What are they going to talk about?" Elisabet wanted to know.

The angel laughed. "They're trying to reach agreement about correct Christian doctrine."

"Are they going to agree?"

"After long discussions, they'll finally make a declaration that Jesus was both God and man. But they're discussing many other things as well. Some of them are so eager to determine the correct belief that in their haste they forget what is most important."

"And what's that?" asked Elisabet.

"That Jesus came into the world to teach people to be kind to one another. No other lesson is more difficult for a human being to learn, but no other lesson is more important. It's not as important, for example, to know how many angels there are in heaven or whether God has a splinter in His little finger."

"Has he *really* got one?"

"It doesn't matter, I told you. It's more important to see the beam in your own eye."

Elisabet thought it was very difficult to understand that answer, but she hid the angel's words in her heart. She would perhaps understand them better another time.

The two Wise Men were not entirely satisfied with what the angel had said. "It is, strictly speaking, not necessary to believe in angels at all." said Caspar. "Many people believe that such concepts have very little to do with what Jesus wished to teach us."

"All the angel stories may only be fairy tales," added Balthazar. "But that Jesus wished to teach humans to be kind to one another is no fairy tale."

Now Ephiriel began to argue. "We angels are not in the habit of using such strong words," he said in a very gentle voice. "All the same, I must say that this is one of the silliest things I've ever heard, at least on this pilgrimage. You should be ashamed of yourselves, both of you. Or you should stay in the Orient and not start wandering west with such irresponsible talk."

"Yes, indeed," added Impuriel. "You should be ashamed of yourselves, both of you. *I'm* offended."

The next moment, Impuriel did something Elisabet thought angels in heaven would never do. He put his hand in front of his offended face and thumbed his nose at the two Wise Men from the Orient!

"Bah to you!" said the cherub. *"Yes, indeed!"*

A certain nervousness began to spread among the godly company. The angel Seraphiel spread his arms to show that he was not carrying any weapons.

"It's easy to lose courage when even your nearest and dearest lose faith in you. But although we can disagree about such important matters of belief, we mustn't under any circumstances quarrel. Now, let's try to forget all the unkind things that have been said and all the unkindness that was thumbed."

Joshua the shepherd was clearly in agreement with the last speaker, for he thumped his crook on the ground and said, "To Bethlehem! To Bethlehem!"

And with that they started moving down through Phrygia.

꩜ ☆

JOACHIM sighed.

"It's silly when grownups quarrel," he said. "But it's even sillier when even the angels in heaven start quarreling."

Papa nodded. "These have always been sensitive matters. It's not the first time people have gotten annoyed because of a discussion about angels."

"But they didn't disagree so very much," protested Mama. "The angels and the Wise Men agreed that the most important lesson Jesus wanted to teach people was that we ought to be kind to one another. And that can, in fact, be much more difficult than believing in angels."

Papa opened the atlas and pointed out Constantinople, which is called Istanbul today, as well as the narrow Bosporus Strait where the Emperor Augustus had taken the pilgrims across by ship.

In the pancake book, he found the old city of Chalcedon, where all the priests had met to discuss what Christian doctrine was. Now the pilgrims were in Asia.

☽ ☆

WHEN Mama came home from work that afternoon, she had a large envelope full of newspaper articles. She had been to the library to get copies of everything that had appeared in the newspapers when Elisabet Hansen disappeared in 1948.

The family sat around the coffee table, reading the old newspaper cuttings. They examined the picture of Elisabet Hansen most carefully. Mama took down the photo of the grownup Elisabet from the mantelpiece and compared the pictures.

Could the two pictures be of the same Elisabet?

"Both of them have fair hair," said Mama. "Don't they both have a slightly pointy nose, too?"

Papa was more interested in the disappearance. As he read the old newspapers, he said, "Her mother was a teacher . . . Her father was a well-known journalist . . . Only her little knitted cap was found when the snow melted a few months later . . . in the woods. Otherwise, the police had no clues at all."

"*They* hadn't read the magic Advent calendar," said Joachim.

"Even if they had, they couldn't have arrested an angel," Papa said, laughing.

After Mama and Papa said good night that evening, Joachim put the light on again. It occurred to him that he hadn't looked at the large picture on the outside of the Advent calendar for several days. That was because most of the doors in the calendar had been opened. So he closed them.

And it happened again!

The picture showed Mary and Joseph leaning over the Baby Jesus in the manger. In the background were the Wise Men and the angels descending through the clouds to tell the shepherds in the fields that Jesus was born.

High up on the left side, there was a picture of two men in fine clothes.

Unlike all the others, they were standing with their backs to the scene. Joachim had seen them many times before, and now he was quite certain that they were supposed to be Quirinius and the Emperor Augustus. But only at this moment did he notice that the Emperor was carrying a shining scepter.

Had he been holding a scepter in his hand ever since Joachim was given the calendar in the little bookstore? Or had the scepter drawn itself in?

❈ DECEMBER 19 ❈

. . . he thought it
was so much fun to throw gifts
through people's windows . . .

ON December 19, there was a picture of a *nisse*, a Christmas elf, in the magic Advent calendar. He had long white hair and a white beard. He was wearing a red cloak and a pointed red hat. On his chest hung a large silver cross set with a red stone.

It was Mama's turn to read.

MELCHIOR

A procession was speeding through Asia Minor one day toward the end of the fourth century.

They traveled across the high plains of Phrygia and passed some salt lakes where the birds can stand on the water. On their long journey they encountered bears, wolves, and jackals. But when a wolf or a bear came running toward them, they always managed to step aside by one or two weeks and avoid the wild animal.

They climbed up through a pass in the high mountain range of Pamphylia, which stretches from east to west along the Mediterranean coast. A few thousand meters above sea level, they saw a figure dressed in green. It was a tall man, sitting like a living landmark at the point where the road began tilting down toward the Mediterranean Sea.

As soon as they noticed the man in green, Caspar and Balthazar began waving and tried to get past the sheep.

"Who's that?" asked Elisabet.

"He must certainly be one of us," said the angel Ephiriel.

The stranger rose and threw his arms around Caspar and Balthazar. "The circle is complete," he announced solemnly.

Elisabet didn't understand this, but then the stranger came over and greeted her. "Welcome to Pamphylia," he said. "My name is Melchior, third Wise Man and King of Egryskulla."

Then Elisabet understood what he had meant by the circle being complete, for now all Three Kings of the Orient were together.

"You have such strange names," she said. "You're Wise Men, Kings of the Orient, and Caspar, Balthazar, and Melchior."

Melchior smiled from ear to ear. "We have even more names. In Greek, we are called Galagat, Magalat, and Sakarin. Some people call us Magi. But it doesn't matter what they call us. We are part of this story on behalf of all people on earth who do not come from the Holy Land."

Elisabet looked up at the angel Ephiriel, and the angel nodded. "That's quite true."

"Of course. One would not tell lies, would one?" Melchior went on. "One would not be a King of the Orient unless one spoke the truth, would one? One would not be particularly wise, either, only seeming-wise."

He was so funny when he talked that Elisabet couldn't help laughing.

He had more to say. "I am so happy that I often want to sing and dance. And I am especially happy at Christmas time, for that's when Jesus was born."

"That's enough," said Joshua, striking a stone with his shepherd's crook. "To Bethlehem! To Bethlehem!"

But Melchior spoke again. "We must greet the Christmas *nisse* first. He lives just below here."

They set off down the steep mountainside toward the Mediterranean. As they ran, Elisabet said, "Is it really true that we're going to greet the Christmas *nisse?*"

Ephiriel pointed down at a town clinging to the side of the mountain. They could only catch a glimpse of the Mediterranean in the background.

"The time is 322. The town is called Myra, and this is where Paul came when he was traveling to Rome to tell the capital of the Roman Empire about Jesus. He founded a Christian community in Myra, too."

"I don't understand what that has to do with the Christmas *nisse*."

But the angel went on, "Two hundred years after Paul came to Myra, a boy called Nicholas was born here. His parents were Christians, and when he was a grown man, Nicholas was elected Pope of Myra. In Myra there lived a girl who was very poor because her father had lost everything he owned. She wanted to get married, but it was quite impossible because she had no money for a dowry. Bishop Nicholas wanted to help the poor girl, but he knew her family were too proud to accept a gift of money."

"Perhaps he could have put some money into her father's bank account," suggested Elisabet.

"Yes, but this was a long time before such things as banks existed. Nicholas did something similar, though. He crept out during the night and threw a bag of gold coins through the family's open window. That way, the young girl was able to marry, after all."

"That was kind of him."

"But that wasn't the end of it. He thought it was so much fun to throw gifts through people's windows that he went on doing it. When he died, many legends were told about him. Later, he came to be known as St. Nicholas. In English, that turned into Santa Claus, and in Norwegian into the Christmas *nisse*. The word *nisse* comes from Nicholas, and so do the names Nils and Klaus."

"Did he have a red suit, a long white beard, and a red knitted cap?"

"Wait and see," said the angel Ephiriel.

The sun had not yet risen. They stopped in front of a low church building in Myra, and as soon as they did, the door opened. Out strode a man with a long red cloak, a long white beard, and a red hat on his head. Around his neck he wore a large silver cross with a red stone in it. He almost looked like a Christmas *nisse*, but Ephiriel whispered in Elisabet's ear that the time was 325 years after the birth of Jesus and those were the clothes that bishops wore at that time.

"It is Bishop Nicholas of Myra," whispered the angel.

Elisabet had an idea. "Does the name have anything to do with myrrh?"

"You do well to ask, for myrrh was one of the three Christmas gifts to the Christ Child," said the angel with a smile. "It's become usual to give gifts at Christmas because of the gifts the Three Wise Men brought to the Christ Child, and because of Bishop Nicholas's generosity."

In his arms, the man held three different caskets. He walked with firm steps toward the Three Kings of the Orient, bowed low, and offered each of them a casket. Caspar's casket was full of shining gold coins. In Balthazar's casket was frankincense, and in Melchior's, myrrh.

"We are on our way to Bethlehem," said Caspar.

Bishop Nicholas laughed so that his beard shook. "Ho, ho! So you must take a few little gifts for the Child in the manger. You absolutely must do that, mustn't you? Ho, ho!"

Since Elisabet was standing in front of a real Christmas *nisse*, she ran right up to him and felt his red cloak. He bent down and lifted her up on his arm. She tugged on his beard to find out whether it was real, and it was.

"Why are you so kind?" she asked.

"Ho, ho!" laughed the man in red again. "The more we give away, the richer we become. And the more we keep for ourselves, the poorer we become. That's the mystery of generosity, neither more nor less. But it's the mystery of poverty, too."

Impuriel clapped. "Well spoken, Bishop!"

Bishop Nicholas continued, "All those who collect treasures upon earth will be very poor one day. But those who have given away all they possess will never be poor. Besides, they have had so much fun that they have always rejoiced. Ho, ho! For the greatest joy on earth is generosity."

"Maybe," said Elisabet. "But first you have to own something to give it away."

At that, the good-natured bishop laughed so heartily that his whole body shook. Elisabet almost became seasick as she sat on his arm.

"Not at all," he said, when he had swallowed enough of his laughter so that there was room in his mouth for speaking as well. "You don't need to own anything at all to feel generosity fizzing in your veins. A little smile is enough, or something you've made yourself."

And with those words he put Elisabet down on the mosaic floor in front of the church.

Joshua thumped his shepherd's crook on the ground. "To Bethlehem! To Bethlehem!"

As they moved off, they could hear the bishop's laughter behind them in the church square.

"Ho-ho! Ho-ho! Ho-ho!"

MAMA looked up from the paper and began laughing as well. It was infectious, and when Joachim burst out laughing, Papa couldn't resist. So all three of them sat there chuckling.

At last Mama said, "I think laughter is like the wildflowers. Both are a part of the glory of heaven that has strayed down to earth. But it's very easy for that kind of thing to spill over."

Before Mama finished reading what was written on the piece of paper, Papa had brought out the historical atlas.

"The names are on the map," he said. "And Paul really did visit a little town called Myra when he was on his way from Jerusalem to Rome."

"Perhaps Elisabet in the photo traveled the same way as Paul," suggested Joachim, "because she went to Rome, too."

"And she had a silver cross with a red stone in it," said Mama. "The Christmas *nisse* did, too."

Papa laughed. Then he went into the living room to get an encyclopedia. He came back reading.

"The Bishop of Myra *was* the very first Santa Claus."

"I must say, history is full of strange connections," said Mama. "It's as if Christmas elves have been jumping up and down all through the centuries."

❧ DECEMBER 20 ❧

. . . something suddenly fell from the sky . . .

O N Sunday, December 20, Joachim was awakened by the alarm clock in Mama and Papa's bedroom. Usually, they hardly ever set the alarm on Sunday. But they were probably afraid Joachim would wake up first and open the magic Advent calendar door without them. In any case, the next moment they were both in the room.

Joachim opened the door with the number 20 on it. They saw a picture of a man lying on the ground looking up at a bright light shining down from heaven.

"That's a strange picture," said Mama.

But Papa was impatient. "Let's read," he said.

Today it was Papa's turn to read.

CHERUBIEL

Aprocession was on its way through Asia Minor. During the third century, it sped through Pamphylia and Cilicia, south of the high Taurus Mountains. It crossed rivers, groves, and mountain plains. Sometimes the pilgrims made their way along steep slopes with old tombs hewn out of rock; sometimes they struggled along the edge of the sea, with the sand kicking up behind them; sometimes they sped through Roman cities, including Attalia, Seleucia, and Tarsus. At Tarsus, they paused and looked around for a few seconds. The angel Ephiriel told them that it was where Paul had been born.

On their journey, the pilgrims passed Roman theaters, sports arenas, harbors, triumphal arches, and temples. Now and again, they saw something that might have been a Christian church.

The route was planned so that they would not attract too much attention. It took them a century to cross the country but they showed themselves only in the gray light of dawn, before people were awake. All the same, here and there they frightened the wits out of a night watchman, or a fisherman setting his nets out early. Usually, they sped on, and the fisherman or the night watchman would be left there, rubbing his eyes. But sometimes Impuriel called to them that they should not be afraid.

A human being doesn't often see one of the angels of the Lord, and even then the sight doesn't last longer than a second or two. Then it's easy to believe you've seen a vision, especially if you're a night watchman who hasn't closed his eyes during the long hours of his shift.

The mysterious procession sped around the Gulf of Alexandretta at the very tip of the Mediterranean. From now on, the way to Bethlehem led south along the eastern coast. They arrived at the Syrian city of Antioch and stopped in front of the town gate.

"We are in the Year of Our Lord 238," said the angel Ephiriel. "This is where Paul's missionary journeys began. We should remember, too, that the word 'Christian' was used for the first time in Antioch."

"But weren't Jesus' disciples Christian?" Elisabet wanted to know.

"Yes and no," replied Ephiriel. "It took a long time for the first Christians to begin calling themselves Christians, and the first time when that happened was in this very city. Before then, the Christians thought of themselves as Jews. Paul was a Jew, too, but on his missionary journeys he found that Romans and Greeks could also believe in Jesus. Paul thought they didn't need to become Jews to believe in Jesus. They didn't need to follow all the old rules in the Book of Moses, either. Because Jesus didn't speak to the Jews alone. He had something to say to all people."

The Wise Men came up to Ephiriel.

"We are Wise Men from the Orient," said Caspar, "and Kings of Nubia, Sheba, and Egryskulla. None of us are Jewish. All the same, we are among the very first to welcome the Christ Child into the world."

Joshua struck his shepherd's crook against the city wall. "To Bethlehem!" he said. "To Bethlehem!"

The procession of pilgrims moved off. Ephiriel said that they were on their way to Damascus, the capital of Syria.

After a while, Ephiriel called to them to stop. They were on a deserted stretch of the old Roman road through Syria. "Here it is," said Ephiriel, pointing at a bright red poppy on the side of the road. "The time is 235 years after the birth of Jesus. Two hundred years ago, a miracle took place here, and it was of great importance for the history of the whole world."

The Three Wise Men lined up and bowed solemnly. To show that he agreed, the Emperor Augustus planted his scepter on the exact spot that the angel had indicated.

The four shepherds tried to collect the little flock of sheep around the Emperor's scepter. It shone like a small sun. Quirinius, who had once been a governor in this country, called their attention to the landscape, saying, "It's good to be home again. Now it's only a couple of hundred years since I was the Governor of Syria."

"Excuse me for asking you so directly," said Elisabet, "but I may be the only person who doesn't understand what you are all talking about. Jesus wasn't born here, was he?"

Ephiriel laughed. "In the Year of Our Lord 35 after Christ, a Jew from Tarsus in Asia Minor was on his way to Damascus. His Roman name was Paul, but his Jewish name was Saul. As a young man he had lived in Jerusalem, where he studied the ancient Jewish scriptures. He may have met Jesus there and listened to what He had to say. But Paul was a Pharisee, and the Pharisees believed that people could appease God by following all the laws and precepts in the Books of Moses. He became one of the enthusiastic persecutors of the Christians. He helped to throw them in prison, and even helped to kill St. Stephen."

"Then he was a big fool," said Elisabet.

Ephiriel and all the others nodded. The angel continued, "But when he was on his way to Damascus to persecute the Christians there, he had a strange experience. Suddenly a light shone down from heaven, and Paul heard a voice saying, 'Saul, Saul, why are you persecuting Me?' Paul asked who was calling him, and the answer was, 'I am Jesus, whom you are persecuting. Arise and go into the city, and you will be told what you must do.' Paul and the men who were with him were struck speechless. All of them had heard the voice, but none of them had seen anything but the light from heaven."

Impuriel nodded. "That's exactly what it was like. The voice they heard didn't even say 'Fear not.'"

"Paul went into Damascus and joined the congregation there. Before long, he became the first great Christian missionary. Paul was a Roman citizen; he spoke Greek and Aramaic, which was the language Jesus spoke. And he could read the scrolls of scripture in Hebrew. On his four missionary journeys, he preached about Jesus in Greece and Rome, Syria and Asia Minor."

As Ephiriel was speaking, something suddenly fell from the sky. It happened so quickly that Elisabet didn't even have time to jump. At first she thought it was a bird that had fallen to earth because it had forgotten to beat its wings. Then she saw that another angel was standing in front of her.

"Fear not," said the angel. "I am Cherubiel and I shall accompany you on the last stage of your journey to Bethlehem."

The Emperor Augustus picked up the scepter he had set in the spot where Paul had heard the voice from heaven, the shepherds gave the sheep a little push, and Joshua called out, "To Bethlehem! To Bethlehem!"

PAPA let the piece of paper fall on the bed. "Amazing!" he said.

He opened the atlas to show how the country they traveled through had looked in the third century after Christ. Then he repeated all the names and pointed to them on the map. It was almost as if he were singing: "Pamphylia, Cilicia, Attalia, Seleucia, Tarsus, Antioch."

Since it was Sunday, they had plenty of time. They had started getting ready for Christmas: washing the linens and the floors, baking cakes, and coloring marzipan sweets. That day, Mama and Papa also read old atlases and encyclopedias. They wanted to know more about the places the pilgrims had passed through.

"I feel as if I'm back at school," Mama said, laughing.

Papa read aloud from a book in the Bible called the Acts of the Apostles, where there was a lot about Paul.

"I've found it," he said. " 'While he was still on the road and nearing Damascus, suddenly a light flashed from the sky all around him. He fell to the ground and heard a voice saying, 'Saul, Saul, why are you persecuting me?' And he said, 'Who are You, Lord?' And the Lord said, 'I am Jesus, whom you are persecuting. Arise and go into the city, and you will be told what you have to do.' And the men who journeyed with him stood speechless, hearing a voice but seeing no one. Then Saul arose from the ground, and when his eyes were opened he saw no one. But they led him by the hand and brought *him* into Damascus. And he was three days without sight, and neither ate nor drank.' "

It was strange for Joachim to see Papa sitting in the green rocking chair, reading the Bible.

Once he put the heavy book down in his lap and said, "This book is really just as remarkable as the magic Advent calendar."

Joachim was eating his supper when the phone rang. Mama answered it. She gave the receiver to Papa.

"Yes," Papa said. "Speaking . . . Of course, it happened many years ago . . . No, I understand that . . . Yes, it's a clear picture . . . Quite certain . . . It's St. Peter's Basilica in the background . . . I would never have given up hope, either . . . No, I wouldn't . . . All we have is this strange calendar that came to us by chance . . . He's disappeared . . . No, I've never met him . . . My family say that, too . . . Pointy nose, yes . . . No, I don't believe in angels . . . Not at all . . . Of course, it's possible that she was kidnapped . . . No, but somebody or other . . . I don't know . . . But clearly it's possible that she's still alive . . . She'd be unlikely to remember anything . . . She was only seven . . . Not that old, you say? . . . We have just the one boy . . . No, I would never have given up hope . . . At once, yes . . . I promise . . . And thank you for calling."

He put down the receiver.

"Was that John?" asked Joachim.

Papa shook his head. "It was Mrs. Hansen, Elisabet's mother. I sent her a copy of that old photo. She said the young woman could well be her daughter who disappeared forty-five years ago. But then she was only six or seven years old. She had another daughter right after. Her name's Anna, and she looks a little like the young woman in front of St. Peter's . . ."

When Papa came in to say good night that evening, he stood for a while staring into the darkness outside the window. "What on earth do you think has happened to John?"

"He's out in the wilderness," said Joachim. "But it's not Christmas yet."

21

❄ DECEMBER 21 ❄

. . . the lake looked like a blue china bowl
rimmed in gold . . .

PAPA woke Joachim early on Monday morning, the twenty-first of December.

"We have to get moving," he said. "I have to go to work a little early today, you see. But this is important, too. Maybe it's even more important than my job."

Joachim sat up in bed and opened the proper door. He had almost begun to dread Christmas, because then there wouldn't be anything left of the calendar.

That day, there was a picture of a village beside a shining lake. The village and the low hills around the lake were bathed in gold.

Joachim began to read.

EVANGELIEL

Early one morning at the end of the second century after Christ, the companions raced at top speed into Damascus on the Barada River. They sped past two soldiers who were guarding the western gate and went in along the straight street that cuts right through the city.

The soldiers turned to each other in confusion.

"What was that?"

"A gust of wind from the northwest."

"But it wasn't just wind and sand. I thought I saw people, too."

The two soldiers were reminded of an old story from a few years ago, about something that had happened at the eastern gate. A group of soldiers had been knocked over by a procession that had approached along the main street and thundered out through the city gate. It had consisted of people and animals, and one of the soldiers thought he had seen angels as well.

For as Elisabet, Ephiriel, and the others rushed out through the eastern gate, they happened to bump into some Roman soldiers. The soldiers fell down, picked themselves up in confusion, and tried to see where the procession had gone. But it was already many miles and many years away.

Late in the afternoon one day in the middle of the second century, they came to the Lake of Gennesaret in Galilee. They stopped in front of a village and looked out across the glimmering water.

The hills lay like a wreath around the lake, and with the golden evening sun shining on them, Elisabet thought the lake looked like a blue china bowl rimmed in gold.

The village consisted of simple houses, each with a small shed at one end for the livestock. Between the houses walked laden donkeys led by men wearing tunics and cloaks. Women in flowing robes were carrying jars on their heads.

"We are in Capernaum, which is on the old caravan trail between Damascus and Egypt," explained Ephiriel. "Here Jesus called His first disciples. One of them was the customs official, Matthew, for Capernaum was an important customs station. The brothers Simon Peter and Andrew were two others; they were both fishermen. 'Follow me,' said Jesus, 'and I will make you fishers of men.' "

"He helped them to catch ordinary fish, too," Impuriel hastened to add. "Yes, indeed!"

Ephiriel nodded. "Once, when Jesus was standing by the lake to speak to a large crowd of people, He saw two boats farther down the beach. One of them belonged to Simon Peter. Jesus got on Peter's boat and asked him to set out, and He talked to the crowd from the boat on the lake. That was a good idea, because then all the people could see Him as He spoke. When He finished speaking, He asked Simon Peter to row farther out and cast his nets there. Peter said he had fished all night and not caught a single fish. All the same, he did as Jesus asked, and he caught so many fish that the net broke from the weight."

"Another time, they were out on the lake," Impuriel said. "Suddenly

181

a storm blew up, and the disciples were terrified of drowning. But Jesus just lay down and slept. In the end, He had to quiet the storm so as to calm the disciples."

"He was showing them that they had very little faith," explained Ephiriel.

Impuriel nodded vigorously. "Yes, indeed! Yet another time, the disciples were out on the lake alone, when Jesus came toward them, walking on the water. When the disciples saw Him, they were scared; they thought He was a ghost or something. But when Simon Peter saw it was Jesus, he thought he'd show off, to prove how great his faith was. So he stepped out of the boat and walked on the water, too. It went well at first, but in a short time he became afraid of the waves and began to sink. He called to Jesus to come and save him."

Joshua struck his shepherd's crook against a pile of broken stones. "To Bethlehem! To Bethlehem!"

They sped off along the shore of the Lake of Gennesaret. Before long, Ephiriel called to them to stop. He pointed up at a shelf in the rock.

"That's where Jesus gave the famous Sermon on the Mount. He talked about the most important things He wanted to teach us."

"What were they?" Elisabet wanted to know.

Impuriel spread his wings, jumped up in the air, and said, "Our Father, Who art in heaven! Hallowed be Thy name. Thy Kingdom come. Thy will be done on earth as it is in heaven . . ."

Here he was interrupted by Ephiriel. "Yes, He taught them to pray. Above all, He wanted to teach human beings to be kind to one another. But He also wanted to show that nobody is perfect in the sight of God but that it's all right."

" 'Blessed are the merciful,' " said Impuriel. " 'Whosoever shall smite thee on thy right cheek, turn to him the other also . . . Love your enemies and pray for those who persecute you . . . Whatsoever ye would that men should do to you, do ye even so unto them . . .' "

"That's enough, thank you!" interrupted Ephiriel. "We know you remember it all. I should hope so, as one of the angels of the Lord."

All Three Wise Men obviously wanted to say something. Caspar and Balthazar nodded at Melchior and let him speak.

"But it's not enough to learn the rules of life by heart. It's more important to try to follow them. And the most important thing is to do something for people in need, for people who are sick and poor, and for people fleeing from their homes. That is the message of Christmas."

"To Bethlehem!" called Joshua again. "To Bethlehem!"

They had scarcely gotten up speed when Ephiriel turned to Elisabet and told her that they were running through the place where Jesus had fed five thousand people with only a few loaves and fishes.

"Yes, indeed!" exploded Impuriel. "Jesus wanted people to share the little they had. If only they could learn to share with each other, nobody would be hungry or poor."

When they came to the village of Tiberias, they turned from the Lake of Gennesaret and up through a hilly area. At the head of a fertile valley with palms and fruit trees was another village.

Ephiriel called to the procession to stop. "Angel time says 107 years have passed since Jesus was born. This town is called Nazareth. Jesus grew up here, the son of Joseph the carpenter. This was where an angel of the Lord appeared to Mary to tell her she was going to have a child."

He had scarcely finished speaking when something fell down through a hole in the sky. The next moment, still another angel was standing in front of the pilgrims. In his hand he held a trumpet. The angel blew once on the trumpet and said, "I am the angel Evangeliel, and I proclaim to you a great joy. There is only a short time left until Jesus is born."

Impuriel began fluttering around Elisabet. "He is one of us and will be with us on the last part of our journey to Bethlehem."

Elisabet was reminded of the words to an old Christmas carol.

> The angel of the Lord came down,
> And glory shone around

she sang in as pretty a voice as she could.

The Three Wise Men clapped their hands because she sang so beautifully.

That embarrassed her. So that they would not just look at her, she said, "We must be getting close to Bethlehem, since there are so many angels here."

Joshua gave one of the sheep a little slap on its rump. "To Bethlehem! To Bethlehem!"

Now there were only a hundred years to go before they reached the city of David.

☽ ☆

"NOW things are starting to fall into place," Papa said.

Mama turned toward him in surprise. "You mean, they've arrived in the Holy Land?"

Papa shook his head. "Quirinius said something yesterday when they were

184

approaching Damascus. 'It's good to be home again,' he said. Naturally, that was because the Governor of Syria may well have lived in Damascus. But I seem to hear John's voice: 'It's good to be home again.' "

"You mean John made the magic Advent calendar and he really does come from Damascus?" Joachim said.

Papa nodded. "Who is Quirinius in this extraordinary story? It was Quirinius who gave Elisabet an Advent calendar, the one with the picture of the fair-haired girl. That's how he's imagined himself into the story he's telling, he and the young woman he met in Rome. He's put it into the middle of this long story. Although Quirinius and that Advent calendar only come in the twelfth and thirteenth chapters, Quirinius has said 'Dixi' all the time when he has something to say. That means 'I have spoken'—and I hear John's voice again. He has spoken, and what he has said is in this remarkable Advent calendar."

"You're right," said Mama.

"But an interesting piece of information came out today," Papa went on.

"What?" asked Mama and Joachim together.

"The old flower seller has described many towns and places on the long journey to Bethlehem. But today the description was more exact. He writes about the straight street that cuts right through Damascus from the western to the eastern gate. Only someone familiar with the place would write like that."

"Perhaps so," said Mama. "But don't you think he might have heard the old story about the soldiers who were knocked over by a procession of angels?"

"Nonsense!" Papa said, snorting.

Then he stopped himself. "But nothing can be discounted. If only we could find him!"

Joachim was thinking about something very different. He looked down at the piece of paper he'd been reading from, put his finger on one of the sentences, and said, "The Wise Man said it's important to do something for people who are fleeing from their homes. What do you think he meant by that?"

"I suppose he was thinking of refugees and people like that," Papa said.

"Exactly!" said Joachim. "That's just what I thought."

"What about it?" asked Mama.

"I thought it had something to do with the lady in the photo. *She* was a refugee. And she was his girlfriend."

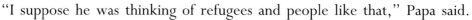

BEFORE Joachim fell asleep that evening, he spent a little time playing with the letters of the alphabet. He thought about John, who had met Elisabet in Rome, and about Roma, which turned into a word that meant love when he read it backward.

Finally, he wrote some magic letters in his little notebook:

```
E L I S A B E T
L           E
I   R O M A B
S   O   M A
A   M   O S
B   A M O R I
E           L
T E B A S I L E
```

The diagram looked like a door—or perhaps a door that was inside another door. But what was inside *that* door?

22

❧ DECEMBER 22 ❧

. . . his food was locusts and wild honey . . .

JOACHIM woke up early on the morning of December 22. There were only three days left to Christmas—and only three doors left to open in the magic Advent calendar. He was excited about what he would find out when he opened the last doors in the magic Advent calendar. But he didn't dare do anything before Mama and Papa got up.

There they were, both of them.

Joachim opened the door and saw a picture of a man standing in a river, the water up to his waist. The upper part of his body was clothed in rags.

Mama unfolded the piece of paper and read.

THE INNKEEPER

A godly band was journeying through Samaria. It was at the very end of the first century after Jesus' birth.

In the gray dawn one day in the year 91, they stopped by the banks of the River Jordan, which runs from the Lake of Gennesaret to the Dead Sea.

"Here it is!" called Ephiriel.

The angel Seraphiel went on. "Out here in the wilderness Jesus was baptized by John the Baptist. John wore a camel's-hair cloak, with a leather belt around his waist. His food was locusts and wild honey."

"I know that," said Impuriel, "for John had said, 'I indeed baptize you with water: But One mightier than I is coming, whose sandal strap I am not worthy to loose. He will baptize you with the Holy Spirit and with fire.' Then Jesus came and allowed himself to be baptized in the River Jordan. I was sitting high up above in the clouds, clapping my hands. It was a great moment."

"Wasn't that when a dove came down from heaven?" Elisabet wanted to know. She thought she had heard something like that once.

Impuriel beat his wings and nodded. "Yes, indeed!"

"To Bethlehem!" said Joshua. "To Bethlehem!"

"How far is it to Bethlehem?" Elisabet asked.

"Not very far at all!" said Impuriel.

They began running again and were soon passing a large city. As they ran, Ephiriel said that the city was called Jericho and was possibly the oldest city in the whole world.

They hurried on along the ancient road between Jericho and Jerusalem. It was the road where the Good Samaritan had helped the poor man who had been attacked by thieves.

They whirled up to Jerusalem. First they climbed up to the Mount of Olives. They looked down at Gethsemane, where Jesus had been taken prisoner, and his disciples had slept when they should have been watching with Him. When they looked out over Jerusalem, Elisabet could see only ruined buildings. Could this be the Jewish capital?

"The angel watch says it's the year 71 after Christ," explained Ephiriel. "Barely a year ago, the Romans sacked Jerusalem and destroyed the city because its people had rebelled against the Roman colonial power. Today the Eternal City resembles shattered pottery."

"It was the Emperor Titus who did it," said Impuriel. "Not just him alone, of course. It was Titus and his soldiers."

"They destroyed the temple as well," continued Ephiriel. "Only a small part of the west wall is left. Later, this wall will be called the Wailing Wall. From this time on, the Jews will be scattered over the whole world."

"It's so sad it almost makes me cry," whimpered Impuriel. "We keep on saying 'Peace be with you' and 'Peace on earth.' But humans never seem to learn that they must not fight. Though one of the last things Jesus said before he was taken prisoner was that those who live by the sword shall perish by the sword."

Ephiriel agreed. "All those who celebrate Christmas must remember that, because peace is the message of Christmas."

"That's what we sing every Christmas Eve," continued Impuriel. "We sing, 'Glory to God in the highest and peace on earth!' But it's just as if people don't want to listen to that hymn. Soon I won't bother to sing it anymore, so there."

Joshua struck his shepherd's crook on the very top of the Mount of Olives and said, "To Bethlehem! To Bethlehem!"

They sped through the city. A few people were moving among the ruins. One woman was looking in the ramshackle buildings as if searching for something she had lost.

The pilgrims ran through the remnants of the western city gate and down the road to Bethlehem. They were only a few kilometers from the city of David.

All of a sudden, they saw a man who was walking beside an ass. When he heard the procession approaching, he looked up and waved both arms.

"Fear not! Fear not!" shouted Impuriel from a long way away.

But the man was not in the least afraid.

"Then he is one of us," said Ephiriel.

The man and the ass came toward them. He offered his hand to Elisabet. "I am the innkeeper. I am the one who will say that there's not room for

Mary and Joseph. But I shall lend them the stable." Whereupon he lifted Elisabet onto the back of the ass. "You must be tired after your long journey," he said.

Elisabet shook her head. "I've run through the whole of Europe, and I've run through the whole of history as well. It goes just as quickly as if you're running down an escalator."

The man stared at her without understanding. "Did you say escalator?"

Joshua struck his crook on the ground. "To Bethlehem! To Bethlehem!"

☽ ☆

MAMA looked at the others with a solemn expression on her face. She nodded once or twice, and Papa said, " 'Out here in the wilderness Jesus was baptized by John the Baptist.' "

"I know that," said Joachim, exactly like the angel Impuriel in the magic Advent calendar. He went on, excitedly, "John the flower seller is out in the wilderness, too. Besides, he poured water over himself and over the bookseller. *Yes, indeed!*"

"That can't be accidental, can it?" said Papa. "And we never thought about his name!"

"People and flowers both need water," Joachim went on. "In the magic Advent calendar it says that the wildflowers are part of the glory of heaven that has strayed down to earth. I expect there was a lot of the glory of heaven in the River Jordan, too."

Papa got to his feet and went into the living room to get the Bible. When he came back, he turned the pages backward and forward. Then he read aloud:

The voice of one crying in the wilderness:
Prepare the way of the Lord,
Make His paths straight.
Every valley shall be filled,
And every mountain and hill brought low;
And the crooked places shall be made straight
And the rough ways made smooth;
And all flesh shall see the salvation of God.

"In a way, this is what the Advent calendar is trying to tell us," said Papa. "The pilgrims have been traveling toward Bethlehem, but they have also seen how the stories about Jesus have spread across the whole world."

"Perhaps so," said Mama. "But I won't be satisfied until we've solved the mystery of who Elisabet the first is, and the second, and the third."

They had to hurry to work and to school. Joachim had to go to the Christmas pageant in the gym. His class was performing the Nativity play for the other students.

On his way home, the thought came to him that nearly all the pilgrims who had taken part in the long pilgrimage in the magic Advent calendar had taken part in the school Nativity play as well.

As he was letting himself into the house, he noticed a letter stuck in the crack on the door. He pulled it out. It was addressed: "To Joachim"!

He hurried inside and sat down on the bench in the hall. He opened the letter and read:

Dear Joachim,
    I am inviting myself for a cup of coffee and a Christmas cookie or two on December 23 at 7 p.m. I hope the whole family will be there.
    Yours, John

Mama arrived before long, but Joachim waited until Papa came home to tell them about the letter from John. They were sitting at the dinner table.

"I've had a letter from John today," he began. He had to struggle to keep back a big smile.

"What?" Papa nearly choked. He stood up and held out his hand. "Let's see!"

He must have forgotten that it is wrong to read other people's letters.

But Joachim ran to his room to get the letter. He gave it to Papa, and Papa read it aloud to Mama.

Mama gasped. "Tomorrow at seven? We have to be here!"

Papa grinned from ear to ear. "For a Christmas cookie or two! We'll put out everything we've got—including the marzipan cake. Because it's Christmas!"

23

❦ DECEMBER 23 ❦

. . . it was as if
they were all rehearsing something they had
to know by heart . . .

IT'S Christmas! thought Joachim when he woke on December 23. He was itching to open the last door but one in the magic Advent calendar. But he didn't dare touch it until Mama and Papa came in.

Before long, both of them were there. Papa said he had taken a day off work.

"Because it's Christmas," he repeated.

Joachim opened the last door but one in the Advent calendar. It was a picture of a man walking beside an ass. On the ass sat a woman in red.

A folded piece of paper fell out of the calendar. It was Papa's turn to read. Joachim could see his hand was shaking.

MARY AND JOSEPH

A godly company was on its way to Bethlehem. In a way, the procession of pilgrims stretched from the long, narrow countries below the cold North Pole at the top of Europe, right down to warm Judea, which is where Europe, Asia, and Africa meet. It stretched from the distant future right back to the beginning of our era.

There were seven godly sheep, four shepherds, three Kings of the Orient, five angels of the Lord, the Emperor Augustus, the Governor Quirinius, the innkeeper, and Elisabet, who was allowed to sit on the back of an ass on the last part of the journey to the city of David.

They moved along more and more slowly. Soon they were going at an ordinary walking pace. Ephiriel said the angel watch had stopped at the year 0. He pointed to a city far away and said that was Bethlehem.

At once, the Emperor Augustus halted and planted his scepter in the ground under an olive tree. He stood straight, opened the book he had been carrying under his arm, and said in a commanding voice, "The time has come!"

They all remained standing on the road, and the Emperor continued solemnly: "I order you all to write your names in the census."

He held up a piece of charcoal and handed it to each of the pilgrims in turn. Then they all wrote their names in the big book. Only the sheep were excused, probably because they couldn't write and because nobody had given them names.

Elisabet was the last to write her name. She read out all the other names before she added her own signature.

1st shepherd: Joshua

2nd shepherd: Jacob

3rd shepherd: Isaac

4th shepherd: Daniel

1st Wise Man: Caspar

2nd Wise Man: Balthazar

3rd Wise Man: Melchior

1st angel: Ephiriel

2nd angel: Impuriel

3rd angel: Seraphiel

4th angel: Cherubiel

5th angel: Evangeliel

Quirinius, Governor of Syria

Augustus, Emperor of the Roman Empire

Innkeeper

Elisabet added her own name in this way:

Then she had a clever idea. Even though the sheep couldn't write and hadn't been given any names, she thought they should be included in the census anyway. She wrote:

1st sheep

2nd sheep

3rd sheep

4th sheep

5th sheep

6th sheep

7th sheep

She glanced up at the Emperor Augustus. She was a little afraid that he might be angry because she had spoiled his census. But he just put away the census.

Elisabet had worked out that there were 23 pilgrims listed in the census if she included herself and the seven sheep. That was as many as a whole class in school.

After they had registered, the pilgrims became a little more solemn than they had been in Copenhagen and Hamelin, in Venice and Constantinople, in Myra and Damascus.

Ephiriel said, " 'And Joseph also went up from Galilee, out of the city of Nazareth, into Judea, to the city of David, which is called Bethlehem, because he was of the house and lineage of David, to be registered with Mary, his betrothed wife, who was with child.' "

The procession of pilgrims moved off slowly. But before long Ephiriel said they had to stop again. He pointed down the road. A young man was walking beside an ass, and on the ass sat a woman in red. In the background, Bethlehem was spread out over a terraced landscape, with long slopes almost bare of grass because of all the flocks of sheep.

"There are Mary and Joseph," said Ephiriel. "For now the time has come; it is like a ripening fruit."

The innkeeper's face took on a busy expression. "I must hurry to get there before them," he said.

He started running over the hills. As he ran, he muttered to himself, "No, I'm sorry, we're full. But you can stay in the stable . . ."

A certain nervousness transmitted itself to the other pilgrims. It was as if they were all rehearsing something they had to know by heart.

Impuriel leaped into the air, beat his wings, and said, " 'Do not be afraid, for, behold, I bring you good tidings of great joy which shall be to all people. For there is born to you this day in the city of David a Saviour, who is Christ the Lord. And this *will be* the sign to you: You will find a Babe wrapped in swaddling clothes, lying in a manger.' "

Ephiriel nodded, and Impuriel exclaimed, "Glorious!"

Then the angel Evangeliel blew his trumpet, and all five angels sang in chorus: " 'Glory to God in the highest, And on earth peace, goodwill toward men.' "

The sheep had suddenly started bleating. It was as if they, too, were practicing something they had to know by heart.

Joshua turned to the other shepherds. " 'Let us now go to Bethlehem and see this thing that has come to pass, which the Lord has made known to us.' "

Then the Wise Men spoke. " 'Where is He who has been born King of the Jews? For we have seen His star in the East and have come to worship Him.' "

They knelt down and held out the caskets with gold, frankincense, and myrrh.

The angel Ephiriel nodded with pleasure. "I think that'll do."

Joshua rested his shepherd's crook carefully on the fleece of one of the sheep and said softly, "To Bethlehem! To Bethlehem!"

☽ ☆

PAPA had read that a certain nervousness had spread among the pilgrims as they came closer to the stable in Bethlehem. The same thing happened in Joachim's room.

"There must be only one Advent calendar like this in the whole world," said Papa, "and we're the only people to have been given it."

Mama nodded. "And the real Christmas night happened only once, but that night spread Christmas across the whole world."

"That's because the glory of heaven spreads so easily," said Joachim. "I think it must be infectious."

There was still a lot to do before Christmas. The family tradition was that Mama and Papa decorated the tree on the evening of the twenty-third, after Joachim had gone to bed. But this year they decided they would all three do it before John came. Then everything would be ready for Christmas.

Afternoon came. Mama set the table and she put out all the good things they had to eat, including the big marzipan cake.

The clock was striking seven when the doorbell rang.

"You open it, Joachim," said Mama. "You were given the magic Advent calendar, and he sent his letter to you."

Joachim ran to the door. The old flower seller was standing on the steps. He was smiling. In his hands, he held a bouquet of roses.

"Please come in," said Joachim.

Then Mama and Papa came and John gave Mama the roses.

"Thank you very much," she said, "and thank you for the wonderful Advent calendar."

John put his hand on Joachim's head and replied modestly, "I think perhaps I ought to thank *you*."

When they were seated, John took a sip of coffee and began to tell them about himself. "I was born in Damascus and grew up there. Some people think our family goes back to the first Christian congregation in Syria. One day when I was a boy, I found an old jar with some scrolls that were almost in shreds. My parents had the good sense to take the jar with the manuscripts to the museum. There they discovered that the jar was very old. So were the scrolls."

"What was written on the scrolls?" Papa asked.

"They were various reports from Roman legionaries. Among other things, they told of something that happened in Damascus at the end of the second century after Christ. In the year 175, a curious procession is supposed to have come rushing out through the eastern city gate. A few years later, a similar procession came rushing *into* the city through the western gate. There were some angels in both processions."

Mama and Joachim nodded, for they remembered what they had read in the magic Advent calendar.

"There are many legends and myths like that from times gone by," continued John, "but I was surprised that the procession should have run *out* of the city *before* it ran *into* the city. It would have had to be running back in time, and that's impossible, of course.

"But my interest in myths and legend had been awakened," John continued. "I began to read old books, and was particularly interested in stories about people who thought they had seen angels. Finally, I had a good collection of such stories, from my own part of the world and from many countries in

Europe. After some years, I went to Rome to make use of the treasures in the libraries there."

"And that's where you met Elisabet?" Joachim asked.

John nodded.

"But wait a bit. I had paid attention only to a few of the angel stories, because I thought they had something in common. They were from widely differing places, such as Hanover and Copenhagen, Basle and Venice, the Val d'Aosta in northern Italy and the Axios Valley in Macedonia. And they were from very different periods, too. The earliest story was from Capernaum in Galilee, and the latest was from Norway—*that* happened on a country road outside Halden as recently as 1916."

"The vintage car!" said Joachim.

"Of course, there are very few people who believe such stories these days. All the stories I had collected indicated that the sight of the little girl and the angel had lasted only a second or two. But when I compared the stories from Halden, Hanover, and Hamelin with the stories from Aosta, Axios, and Capernaum—well, those stories became quite remarkable."

The old man sat lost in thought for a while.

"Something that is mysterious for one second is often quenched like an empty oil lamp in the next," he said. "Yet, if only we turn our heads in another direction, a new light may be lighted there. For we cannot take in what is sacred in the same way as we pick up stone from the ground and put it in our pocket. Angels waft down unseen; they don't fall onto the middle of the market square."

"What happened to the young woman in the photo?" asked Papa.

John sighed. Joachim thought he saw a tear in the corner of his eye; in any case, he raised his hand there.

"Once," he said, "many, many years ago, I met a young woman in Rome. It was a meeting which lasted only a few weeks, but I became very fond of her."

"Tell us about it," said Papa.

"She called herself Tebasile and was very secretive. She said she had probably been born in Norway but she had grown up among shepherds and sheep farmers in Palestine. She spoke fluent Arabic. And the name Tebasile sounded Palestinian . . . although it could just as easily have been Italian."

"But it's Elisabet backward!" exclaimed Joachim.

John nodded. "Yes, you are very sharp. People don't usually spell their names backward."

"Go on!" begged Papa.

"It might have been true that she was Norwegian as well. Her skin was fair, almost peach-colored, and her eyes were blue and sparkling. When I asked what took her to Palestine, she just stared into my eyes. She said, 'I was kidnapped . . .' I had to ask who kidnapped her, and she replied, 'An angel who needed me in Bethlehem . . . but it's so long ago . . . I was only a little girl . . .' "

"What did you say, then?" Mama asked.

"Other people would probably have smiled at such a pack of lies. But I thought of all my angel stories. I said that I believed what she told me . . . But the fact that I took her seriously must have scared her."

"What happened?" asked Mama.

"We saw each other only once after that. It was on the Way of Reconciliation in front of St. Peter's Square. She said she would be leaving Rome the same afternoon. But she let me take a picture of her. That was in April 1961."

"How did *you* come to Norway?" asked Papa. "And why?"

John took the top ring of the marzipan cake and said, "I came here because I hoped to find the mysterious woman, and I've stayed. But I've never found her. I've never even learned where she might be. But we'll see . . ."

He took a bite of the marzipan ring. "It wasn't long before I heard about that disappearance in 1948. That was when I began asking myself whether the little girl could have been Tebasile—who had said she was kidnapped by an angel when she was a child. I didn't know exactly how old she was, but it would fit if she had been born around 1940."

John was silent a long while. Then he said, "I noticed the strange similarity in the names only recently. It's a fact that we often repeat in our minds the names of people we think about. One day we suddenly read it backward. During my early years in Norway, I thought about Tebasile almost continually. Then it struck me—like a bolt from the blue. When I read her name backward, it turned into Elisabet! I became even more convinced that I really had found the missing Elisabet many, many years later in Rome. That was when I began to make the magic Advent calendar. It took me many months.

"In any case, it was an incredible coincidence," commented Papa.

"I had to ask myself whether she really could be one and the same person," John said. "After all, it was curious that one name turned into the other name backward. This must have been just after I met Anna, Elisabet's younger sister. It had struck me that Anna was an amusing name that was exactly the same whichever way you read it, from front to back or back to front. Maybe that was why I suddenly spelled Elisabet backward. Besides, I thought Elisabet's little sister was very like Tebasile."

"Why did you make the Advent calendar?" asked Mama. "Why didn't you write it all down in a book?"

John laughed. "Do you think anyone would have believed this story? Who would have published it?"

Mama shook her head, and the old man said, "I made the magic Advent calendar so that at least one person could carry the story of Elisabet and the long pilgrimage further. I hoped that the old mystery might one day be solved. After all, I don't know how much time I have left. But now I'm not the only person who knows the strange story."

"Then you put a picture of Elisabet in the store window," said Mama.

John nodded. "To see if anyone here in town would recognize her."

"Why did you travel to the wilderness?" Joachim wanted to know.

And the old flower seller explained. "Every Advent, I go out to the country and walk in the woods and hills outside town. To find peace before the Christmas feast, but also to see if I can find any trace of the little lamb, Elisabet, and the angel Ephiriel who set off for Bethlehem in 1948. I admit it. Sometimes I walk about saying the two names in my head: Elisabet . . . Tebasile . . . Elisabet."

"Haven't you ever wanted to go back to Damascus?" asked Papa.

John shook his head. "No, this is my home now. I sell flowers at the market, and that way I can help spread a little of the glory of heaven. It's very easy for that kind of thing to spread, you know. And one day Elisabet may come back. Because there's something else . . ."

It was so quiet in the room that they could almost hear dust motes falling to the wooden floor.

John said to Joachim, "All these years, I've tried and tried to find her. But I knew only her first name, or so I believed. To find an Elisabet or a Tebasile only by her Christian name—whether in Rome or in Palestine—well, that's more difficult than to catch a sparrow in your hand. I've been laughed at in embassies and in census offices in quite a few countries. But Joachim . . ."

Again it was completely silent in the room.

"Joachim may have helped me to find her again. So I'm the one to thank *you*."

Joachim looked up at Mama and Papa. He couldn't figure out what John was talking about.

"I think you'll have to explain," said Mama.

"It was Joachim who set me to thinking that maybe she had both names, one her first name and the other her last name. It's strange how lacking in imagination we can be when we're thinking the same thoughts year after year."

Joachim's face lit up. "Elisabet Tebasile!" he said. "Is *that* what she's called?"

They could see tears in the old man's eyes. "There's a telephone number in Rome for someone of that name. But it's not Christmas yet. Tomorrow you will open the last door in the magic Advent calendar."

John got to his feet and said he had to hurry, there was something he had to do. "But maybe I can look at the old Advent calendar one last time?"

Joachim rushed into his bedroom and took the magic Advent calendar down from its hook. When he was back in the living room, he handed the calendar to John, who looked carefully at the picture.

"You have to close all the open doors," explained Joachim.

And that's what John did. He said, "Yes, here they all are. Quirinius and the Emperor Augustus, the angels in the sky and the shepherds in the fields, the Kings of the Orient and Mary, Joseph, and the Christ Child."

"But not Elisabet," said Joachim.

"No, not Elisabet."

They went with John to the door. As he was leaving, he said, "So we'll have to see what this Christmas will bring."

"Indeed, we shall," said Papa. He was obviously relieved to have heard the old man's story.

But John said something more. "You won't open the last door in the Advent calendar until the bells ring Christmas in tomorrow afternoon, will you?"

Mama looked at him. "No-o-o, I suppose not."

"No, we'll have to try to wait," decided Papa.

When John was on the steps outside, he said, "Maybe I'll knock on your door tomorrow as well."

Joachim was delighted. He felt something bubbling and fizzing deep down inside him. That was because John had said that maybe he'd look in tomorrow. For Joachim was not as pleased about everything as Mama and Papa were.

Something was missing, it seemed to him.

❧ DECEMBER 24 ❧

*. . . a spark from
the great beacon behind those weak lanterns
in the sky . . .*

CHRISTMAS Eve started out as usual. There was always some last-minute thing that had to be taken care of, some last-minute presents that had to be wrapped. Now and then, Mama or Papa would come into Joachim's room and glance expectantly at the magic Advent calendar. They had promised not to open the last door until the bells rang Christmas in.

Later in the day, they were preparing Christmas dinner. Before long, the whole house smelled of Christmas. At last, it was five o'clock. Papa opened a window, and they could hear the church bells ringing.

Nobody said anything, but they went into the bedroom and Joachim climbed on the bed and opened the last, big door in the calendar. It was the one that covered the manger with the Christ Child. The picture under it showed a cave in a mountain.

For the last time, they sat on the edge of the bed. Joachim read aloud to Mama and Papa.

THE CHRIST CHILD

It's the middle of the world where Europe, Asia, and Africa meet. It's the middle of history at the beginning of our era. Soon it will be the middle of the night as well.

A silent crowd is moving among the houses in Bethlehem. There are a little flock of seven sheep, four shepherds, five angels of the Lord, three Kings of the Orient, one Roman Emperor, the Governor of Syria, and Elisabet from the long, narrow country below the North Pole.

The weak glow of oil lamps streams from the windows in a few of the simple houses, but most people in the old town have gone to bed for the night.

One of the Wise Men points up at the sky, where the stars are burning in the darkness. They are like sparks from a beacon far away. One star is shining more brightly than all the other stars. It looks as if it's hanging a little lower in the sky as well.

> O little town of Bethlehem,
> How still we see thee lie,
> Above thy deep and dreamless sleep

The silent stars go by,

But in thy dark streets shineth

The everlasting light.

The hopes and fears of all the years

Are met in thee tonight,

sings Elisabet softly.

The angel Impuriel turns toward the others, puts a finger to his lips, and whispers, "Hush . . . Hush . . . "

The procession of pilgrims gathers in front of one of the town's inns. In a moment or two, the innkeeper appears at the window. When he sees the group, he nods firmly and points to a cave in the face of the rock.

The angel Ephiriel whispers something; it sounds like the words of a nursery rhyme.

" 'And while they were there, the time came for her child to be born, and she gave birth to her son, her firstborn. She wrapped him in swaddling clothes, and laid him in a manger, because there was no room for them in the inn.' "

They steal across the yard and stop in front of the cave. The smell from it tells them that it is a stable.

Suddenly the silence is broken by the cry of a child.

It is happening now. It is happening in a stable in Bethlehem.

Over the stable, a star is twinkling. Inside the stable, the newborn child is wrapped in swaddling clothes and laid in a manger.

This is a meeting of heaven and earth. For the child in the manger is also a spark from the great beacon behind those weak lanterns in the sky.

This is the wonder. It is a wonder every time a new child comes into the world. This is how it is when the world is created anew under heaven.

A woman is breathing hard and weeping. Not out of sadness. Mary is weeping quietly, deeply, happily. But the child's cries drown her out. The Christ Child is born. He has been born in a stable in Bethlehem. He has come to our poor world.

The angel Ephiriel turns solemnly toward the other pilgrims and says, " 'Unto you is born this day in the city of David a Saviour.' "

The Emperor Augustus nods. "And now it's our turn. Everyone is to take up his or her place, everyone must remember his or her lines."

At a sign from the Emperor, Quirinius speaks. "Shepherds! Take your flock out into the fields, and never forget to be Good Shepherds. Wise Men! Depart to the desert and mount your camels. May you never cease to read the stars in the sky. Angels! Fly high above the clouds, all of you. Do not reveal yourselves to people on earth unless it is absolutely necessary, and never forget to say, 'Fear not!' For there is born to you this day in the city of David a Saviour, who is Christ the Lord."

The next moment, all the shepherds and sheep, the angels and the Wise Men, have vanished. Elisabet is left alone with Quirinius and the Emperor Augustus.

"I must hurry home to Damascus," said Quirinius, "for I have an important role to play there."

"And I must go back to Rome," said Augustus.

Before they left, Elisabet pointed to the stable and asked, "Do you think I may go in?"

The Emperor smiled from ear to ear. "Of course you are to go in. That is *your* role."

Quirinius nodded energetically. "You haven't come all this long way just to hang around out here."

With those words, the two Romans started running back the way they had come.

Elisabet looked up at the starry sky. She had to tilt her head far back to see the big star which was shining so brightly. Again she heard the cry of a child from inside the cave.

So she went into the stable.

☽ ☆

PAPA got up from the bed. "Well, we certainly took a remarkable Advent calendar home with us this year," he said.

He seemed to be finished with it all.

Joachim wasn't as pleased as his father was. What had happened to Elisabet? Mama sat for a while, thinking. When she got to her feet at last, she said, "Christmas dinner will be ready soon. Perhaps you could put the presents under the tree while we're waiting. Because there *are* a few small surprises this year."

Then the doorbell rang. It was Joachim who opened it, and old John was standing outside. Today he was beaming even more than yesterday. "I've come just to thank you," he said.

Mama and Papa hurried to the door and invited him in. The marzipan cake came out on the table again. Only the top ring was missing. Papa had put a ball of red marzipan in its place. Joachim brought out coffee cups and plates.

They sat around the table and John looked at the three of them, one at a time. He had a sly expression on his face.

"When I drew the large picture on the magic Advent calendar," he said, "I tried to do it so there would always be something new to discover. All God's creation was like that, I thought. The more we understand, the more we see around us. And the more we see around us, the more we understand. So there will always be something new to discover if we only have our eyes and ears open to the remarkable world we live in."

Papa nodded, and John went on, "But I didn't know that the calendar was made so that the person who read the pieces of paper would also solve the old mystery of the little girl who disappeared from town almost fifty years ago."

"Have you found out something more about Elisabet?" asked Joachim.

But there was no time to answer, for the doorbell rang again.

Mama looked at Papa, and Papa looked at Mama.

"You'd better open it, Joachim," said John. "I expect you're the person who has opened all the doors in the magic Advent calendar. Now you must open this last one as well. But you must open it from the inside."

As he went to the door, Joachim noticed that Mama and Papa were holding hands. Surely they weren't afraid that it might be the angel Ephiriel come to visit?

Outside, he found a woman who looked about fifty. She was wearing a red coat and had fair hair with a little gray in it. She gave him a big smile and held out her hand. "Joachim?" she said.

Joachim felt dizzy, but he knew who she was, and he shook her hand. "Elisabet Hansen," he said. "Won't you come in?"

When they went into the living room, Mama and Papa were still holding hands. The old flower seller burst out laughing. Joachim thought he looked a little like Bishop Nicholas in the magic Advent calendar.

Elisabet was left standing in the middle of the room with her red coat over her arm. Around her neck she was wearing a silver cross set with a red stone.

When John at last managed to get hold of himself, he got up from his chair and said, "Perhaps I should introduce you. This is Elisabet Tebasile Hansen— one and the same. I came a few minutes ahead of her, but here she is."

Mama and Papa were totally confused. Just in case, Joachim stood in front of them and flapped his arms. "Fear not!" he said. "Fear not! Fear not!"

Only then did they get up from the sofa to shake Elisabet's hand. Mama took her coat and brought another chair. Papa went to get another coffee cup from the kitchen.

Elisabet Hansen was speaking English. But when they all sat down again, Papa spoke in Norwegian. "I think I must ask for an explanation," he said. "I think I must demand an explanation."

"And I'll give it in Norwegian, for the boy's sake," said John. "Because it's to his credit that we are all here today."

It looked as if the woman with the necklace understood what he was saying, for she looked down at Joachim and smiled.

"Go on!" said Papa.

"When I came to see you yesterday, I already knew that Elisabet was on her way to Norway," the old flower seller began.

"Why didn't you tell us?" said Mama.

John chuckled. Then he said, "You are not supposed to open a Christmas present before Christmas Eve. Besides, I couldn't be sure whether she really would come. I couldn't even be sure *who* would be coming."

Papa was shaking his head. It looked as if he would never stop.

"I don't understand," he said.

So John explained. "It started several days ago when I talked to Joachim on the phone. For many years I've tried to trace either a certain Elisabet or a certain Tebasile—I was convinced that she was one and the same. But it was Joachim who gave me the idea that perhaps Elisabet was using Tebasile as her last name. I called Information in Italy and was given a telephone number in Rome. After a few hours, I managed to get her at home. And it didn't take long for her to remember me from those magic days in April 1961.

"I told her the story of a mother who had lost her child in 1948. That's how I could tell her who she was. She came to town late yesterday evening; she has not set foot here since she disappeared that December day forty-five years ago."

Papa jumped up from the sofa and went to the phone.

"What is it?" asked Mama.

"I promised to phone Mrs. Hansen as soon as I heard anything."

John laughed. "Elisabet stayed with her mother last night. They scarcely closed their eyes, but everything is fine, I assure you."

"Well, I have to call the police then," insisted Papa, "so they can forget that old case about the girl who disappeared."

"That's been arranged as well," replied John. "You can't have read the papers today. You can't have listened to the radio, either. The whole country is delighted."

Papa sank back on the sofa. There was nothing for him to do. He could only sit and listen to the rest of what John had to tell.

"May I ask a question?" he said.

John nodded. "Of course."

"Exactly what *did* happen in December 1948? And don't tell me that Elisabet set off after a little lamb. Don't tell me she met an angel called Ephiriel, either."

He turned to Elisabet and asked her in English. She put a hand to her mouth to hold back an explosion of laughter, and indicated to John that he should answer.

"She always begins to laugh when we talk about that," explained John. "We can't agree. I'll give you Elisabet's explanation first. She thinks the police in this town did a very bad job. But I think we should begin at the other end."

John stood up and began walking back and forth as he spoke. Now and again, he rested his hand on Elisabet's shoulder.

"Elisabet grew up in a little village near Bethlehem. The people there lived off the poor land they tilled, but even this poor land was taken away from them. When I met Elisabet in Rome in the spring of 1961, she had lived in different refugee camps, first in Jordan, afterwards in Lebanon. She went to Rome to plead the refugees' cause. Well, never mind, we can talk about that later. But Elisabet really did go to Bethlehem in December 1948. She came to poor, persecuted people who needed God's help. That's what she meant when she said she had been kidnapped by an angel. She meant she had been kidnapped by someone who wanted to help the people in the villages around Bethlehem.

She grew up there as a shepherd girl, so she was able to pet the soft fleece of the little lambs at an early age—just like Elisabet Hansen in the magic Advent calendar."

Papa interrupted. "So she suddenly disappeared in Rome," he said. "Why didn't she want to see you again?"

"I've asked myself that many, many times in the years that have passed. The answer is that she had to be very careful about who she talked to. That was why she turned her name upside down and took Tebasile for her last. We mustn't forget that there was a war in the country she came from. Elisabet was afraid of being kidnapped again."

"Go on!" said Papa urgently.

"When I told her I believed her angel story, her suspicions were aroused. She was afraid I might be a dangerous person where her own safety was concerned, and for the Palestinian people."

"But wasn't Elisabet Norwegian?" Mama wanted to know.

John nodded. "Yes, she *was* Norwegian. Elisabet thinks she was kidnapped by some very unhappy people who were willing to do almost anything to make the world aware of the suffering of the Palestinians."

"All the same, it was dreadful to kidnap an innocent child," said Mama.

John nodded several times. "Of course, you're right. Elisabet thinks they must have intended to take her back. Perhaps the people who kidnapped her wanted to get her father to write in the papers about all the people who were driven from village to village and finally herded into huge refugee camps outside their own country."

"So why wasn't she taken back?" interrupted Papa.

"Elisabet says she remembers very little until she was looked after by a large family in the tiny village outside Bethlehem."

"And what is *your* explanation?" asked Mama.

"You know what that is," said John.

Joachim was sitting on the edge of his chair. "You think she *did* follow the little lamb with the bell and met the angel Ephiriel in the woods?"

John nodded. "I do."

"No," said Elisabet.

"Yes," said John.

"No," said Elisabet, and laughed.

The others began laughing, too.

"You mustn't start arguing," said Joachim. "I don't think you should thumb your noses at each other, either."

"I believe Elisabet's story," said Papa.

"And what about you?" asked John, looking at Mama and Joachim.

"I believe twenty-four times more in John's story," said Joachim.

"Then I'll have to vote twelve times for John's story and twelve for Elisabet's," decided Mama. "Because I think a few angels have flown to Bethlehem this Christmas. And back here again, for that matter."

"But Joachim is right when he says we mustn't start arguing even though we believe different things," said John. "That's the message of Christmas, too. Maybe it's the greatest of all truths that the glory of heaven is easily shared—at least, if we humans take part in parceling it out. When I wrote on those thin pieces of paper that I folded so carefully and put inside the magic Advent calendar, I had a few clues. I had heard about Elisabet Hansen who disappeared, and I had met Tebasile in Rome. And I had the old angel stories to rely on as well. The rest of it, I had to imagine myself."

Silence fell in the living room.

"You managed that very well," Mama said finally.

John smiled shyly. "The imagination is also a tiny part of the glory of heaven that has strayed down to earth. It, too, can be shared very easily."

"It's amazing," said Mama. "We open the last door in an old Advent calendar and hear about Elisabet who goes into a stable in Bethlehem to welcome the Christ Child into the world. Right afterwards, the same Elisabet rings the doorbell here in our own house. So it seems almost as if this house is the stable where Jesus was born."

She stood and embraced Elisabet. "Welcome back to Norway, dear child," she said.

That was a funny thing to say, since Elisabet was almost twenty years older than Mama.

"Thank you very much," said Elisabet, and she said those words in Norwegian.

A little later, the phone rang. Papa answered, and Joachim knew right away who he was talking to, because he heard Papa say, "We're all overwhelmed . . . The Christmas present of the year, Mrs. Hansen . . . Yes, *now* I believe in angels . . . Here she is . . . and a Merry Christmas . . . a very Merry Christmas to all your family . . ."

Papa nodded to Elisabet and gave her the receiver. She spoke English, so Joachim couldn't understand what she was saying. But he thought it must be strange to talk to your own mother in a foreign language.

Before long, Elisabet and John had to leave. But they would all meet again after Christmas because Mama and Papa and Joachim had been invited to a big Christmas party at Elisabet's family's home.

The guests were escorted to the front door. Outside, it was snowing hard.

Papa asked whether Elisabet could remember any Norwegian from when she was small.

She stood under the light outside as the snow covered her red coat. Suddenly she bent down and stretched out her hand as if trying to catch the dancing snowflakes.

"Little lamb, little lamb, little lamb!" she said.

She bit her lip in alarm and put her hand up to her mouth. The next moment, she started running. A few seconds later, she and the old flower seller were gone.

☽ ☆

LATE that evening, when Joachim was going to bed, he stood for a long time in front of his window, staring out into the Christmas night. There had been a huge new snowfall, but now it was clear enough to see the stars.

Suddenly he saw some figures running by down on the road. It was not so easy to keep his eyes on them, for he could see them only in the light of the streetlamps, and the sight lasted only a second or two.

Joachim thought he had recognized the angel Ephiriel and all the others who had accompanied Elisabet to Bethlehem.

That night, they had escorted her back.